D1463605

Breaking Up with Barrett

THE ENGLISH BROTHERS, BOOK #1
THE BLUEBERRY LANE SERIES

KATY REGNERY

SPENCER
HILL
PRESS

Please visit www.katyregnery.com

First Edition: July 2014
Katy Regnery

Breaking Up with Barrett : a novel / by Katy Regnery—1st ed.
ISBN: 978-1-63392-072-9

Library of Congress Cataloging-in-Publication Data available upon request

Published in the United States by Spencer Hill Press
This is a Spencer Hill Contemporary Romance, Spencer Hill
Contemporary is an imprint of Spencer Hill Press.
For more information on our titles visit www.spencerhillpress.com

Distributed by Midpoint Trade Books
www.midpointtrade.com

Cover design by: Marianne Nowicki
Interior layout by: Scribe, Inc.
The World Of Blueberry Lane Map designed by: Paul Siegel

Printed in the United States of America

The Blueberry Lane Series

THE ENGLISH BROTHERS

Breaking Up with Barrett
Falling for Fitz
Anyone but Alex
Seduced by Stratton
Wild about Weston
Kiss Me Kate
Marrying Mr. English

THE WINSLOW BROTHERS

Bidding on Brooks
Proposing to Preston
Crazy about Cameron
Campaigning for Christopher

THE ROUSSEAUS

Jonquils for Jax
Coming August 2016
Marry Me Mad
Coming September 2016
J.C. and the Bijoux Jolis
Coming October 2016

THE STORY SISTERS

Four novels
Coming 2017

THE AMBLERS

Three novels
Coming 2018

Based on the best-selling series by Katy Regnery,

The World of...

The Rousseaus of Chateau Nouvelle
Jax, Mad, J.C.
Jonquils for Jax • Marry Me Mad
J.C and the Bijoux Jolis

The Story Sisters of Forrester
Priscilla, Alice, Elizabeth, Jane
Coming Summer 2017

The Winslow Brothers of Westerly
Brooks, Preston, Cameron, Christopher
Bidding on Brooks • Proposing to Preston
Crazy About Cameron • Campaigning for Christopher

The Amblers of Greens Farms
Bree, Dash, Sloane
Coming Summer 2018

The English Brothers of Haverford Park
Barrett, Fitz, Alex, Stratton, Weston, Kate
Breaking up with Barrett • Falling for Fitz
Anyone but Alex • Seduced by Stratton
Wild about Weston • Kiss Me Kate
Marrying Mr. English

For Bella, who sat me down and told me:

Write the books.
Write the books.
Write <u>all</u> of the books.

Epic advice.
Thank you.

CONTENTS

Chapter 1

Barrett English.

Emily's heart kicked into a gallop as she looked down at the caller ID on her buzzing phone. Trying to steady her suddenly shallow breathing, she closed her eyes for a brief second before pushing back from the coffee shop table where the rest of her study group continued to discuss early-American industrialization.

"Be right back," she whispered to her roommate, Valeria, and ducked out the backdoor of the café into an empty alley.

"Hello?"

"Mr. English for Miss Edwards?"

"Okay."

A moment later his smooth, polished baritone voice came on the line. "Good afternoon, Emily. Thank you for picking up."

"I was at study group," she said, leaning against a brick wall and cringing at the way she made it sound like his call wasn't welcome.

"I'm sorry to interrupt you."

"N-no. It's fine," she answered quickly, wiping her sweaty hands on her jeans as she sandwiched the phone between her shoulder and ear. Damn it, she wished she could be cooler, but her mind always went blank the moment she heard the low rumble of his voice.

"I'll be brief," he said. "Tomorrow night. The Union League Club. Seven o'clock."

Emily sighed. She had plans tomorrow night with a sensitive, easy-going, doctoral psych student named Chad who'd asked her out more than once. She'd repeatedly turned him down, but Val had insisted that after four months spent at Barrett English's beck and call, Emily needed to go out with someone with whom she actually had a chance.

"Emily?" he prompted.

"How late?"

"Three hours minimum. Possibly four."

Pushing her hand through her straight blonde hair, she knew it would be smart to decline Barrett's request and go out with psych cutie as planned. The arrangement she had with Barrett—while beneficial to her bank account—wasn't doing her social life any favors. Nor her heart, which didn't seem to comprehend that Barrett only called her because she was his employee. Still, she couldn't bring herself to say no to him.

"Engagement ring?" she asked.

"Per usual."

"The Chanel or the Givenchy?"

"As you wish."

"Hair band or chignon?"

"You always look presentable, Emily. I leave the details to you. Smith will pick you up at six forty-five. Are we done?"

"Yes," she answered and the line immediately went dead.

"Good-bye," Emily said wistfully in the quiet of the alley, disappointment making her grimace. She fisted the phone in her hand until the case pinched her skin and shook her from her trance. "See you *tomorrow*! You're *welcome*! By the way, I love you, you *jerk*!"

Her yell caused a flurry of commotion overhead as a flock of pigeons departed in a hurry for safer, quieter lodgings, one of them pausing just long enough to crap on Emily's shoulder with a big, fat plop.

Fantastic. The perfect metaphor for my life.

She stared at the goopy greyish-white spot in surrender before taking a deep, restorative breath, tucking her phone into her jeans and heading back inside to clean her shirt and rejoin her study group.

An hour later, she trudged home beside Valeria, who started scolding her as soon as Emily shared her last-minute plans for tomorrow night.

"So you'll have to reschedule with Chad? Geez, Em, I don't understand why you keep saying yes to Barrett!" said Valeria, turning up her collar. "Why not just say no?"

"He has a way about him." Emily sighed. "I always consider saying no, but I somehow end up saying yes."

Though they'd never been close or intimate, Emily had known Barrett her entire life—well, not really *known* him, because they were from very different parts of Haverford Park, but he'd been a peripheral part of her life since birth. The economic nature of the call she'd just shared with him was textbook Barrett: businesslike, methodical and goal-oriented. Emily somehow knew he wasn't trying to offend her—he was merely taking care of their mutual business as efficiently as possible. It just hurt that he employed efficiency over warmth since it verified what she had suspected for months: Barrett had little to no personal interest in Emily, despite *her* growing feelings for *him*.

Valeria continued in the no-nonsense tone she used when student teaching. "Here's a solution: say no next time. 'No, Barrett, I refuse to play the part of fake fiancée for you. Take a hike.' Three words, Em— TAKE. A. HIKE." Valeria held up three fingers one by one, then tucked them back into the pocket of her pea coat. "Darn, it's cold."

"It's October in Philadelphia," Emily pointed out.

"Don't change the subject."

"Okay, Val. I'll say no next time. Here goes. 'No thanks, Barrett. You don't make me do anything disgusting. You barely say a word to me. I get to dress up in gorgeous clothes I could never afford, have an expensive glass of wine, and enjoy a scrumptious dinner with people who go out of their way to be polite to me. And yes, I'm flat broke *and so is my roommate*, but no thanks, I don't want your one-hundred an hour to play your fake fiancée. Keep it.' How does that sound?"

"Not so smart."

"I rest my case," said Emily, though the case was far from closed in her heart and mind, which feuded in a tightly locked conundrum. Lately, her heart murmured that she should walk away from Barrett before her feelings for him grew any stronger, while her head insisted she couldn't possibly turn her back on the income he offered.

Valeria's voice interrupted her internal struggle. "Why does he need a fiancée anyway?"

"He only told me once and briefly. Some of his business associates and clients like the stability of a family man on the way to the altar, and he feels that a date makes dinner meetings feel more social and run more smoothly."

Emily's role was to smile warmly, laugh softly, and occasionally make a flattering remark about Barrett, which he would accept with a tight smile before refocusing on the business at hand.

"Why you?" asked Valeria.

"My family has worked for his for three generations—four, if you include me. My father is his family's gardener, just like my grandfather and great-grandfather before. My mother's the head housekeeper at Haverford Park. He knows where I come from. He knows I'll behave myself and keep my mouth shut. I've known the English family since I was brought home from the hospital to live in the gatehouse at the foot of their estate." She shrugged. "Me working for Barrett makes sense."

"I still think it's weird," said Valeria, grumbling as she adjusted her backpack. "Doesn't he know about a hundred society girls he could ask to be his fake fiancée?"

Emily shook her head. "Nah. They'd all take it too seriously. They'd get hopeful. They'd hope that what started as a favor would lead to something real."

Unlike you, her head jibed sarcastically, poking with precision at her heart.

"From what you've told me, he's not exactly Prince Charming."

Emily had explained this before, but Valeria had never lived amongst the English family. She didn't understand the breadth and depth of their wealth and influence.

"Forget Prince Charming, Val. Barrett's the oldest son of English & Sons. He buys companies for breakfast and eats them in pieces for lunch. His nickname is 'the Shark,' for heaven's sake! He's smart and driven and stupendously wealthy. For the woman who doesn't require emotional intimacy, that's a whole lot of diamond tennis bracelets."

Valeria nudged Emily's side, and when she looked up, Val smiled at Emily as she waggled her eyebrows suggestively. "Speaking of intimacy, he's also scorching hot."

And don't I know it, Emily thought with a grimace.

All her life, she'd made a quiet study of Barrett's perfection. His tall, lean, muscular body, his burnished blond hair, the clear blue of his eyes that made her breath catch when he occasionally flashed them at her. He was unbelievably gorgeous—as were all of the English brothers—except Barrett was the original. Over six feet tall with a jaw like a superhero, he was more than attractive. He was, as Valeria had pointed out so illustratively, scorching hot.

But, who cares about that, thought Emily in a concerted effort to convince herself she was immune to his movie star good looks even though it was patently untrue, *when he can barely offer me a smile?*

"I *work* for him, Val."

"I wouldn't mind working *under* him."

"Val!" exclaimed Emily, blushing as she swatted her roommate's arm.

"Speaking as a woman and not an employee, isn't there *anything* you like about him?"

Sure, thought Emily unhappily. *Lots.*

The oldest of five brothers, Barrett was the heir apparent to the most prestigious private equity firm in Philadelphia, and by all outward appearances, Barrett's nickname was right on target. He *was* a business shark, dedicated to the financial dominance of English &

Sons. But Emily couldn't help sensing—as she always had—that deep down inside, there was more to Barrett English than business. She had long held the heart-fluttering theory, possibly incorrectly, that someone so passionate in his business life must have the capacity for *other* deep passions, as well.

Honestly, Emily had no good reason for believing this. His behavior to her was always polite, though not especially warm and inviting. He didn't make Emily laugh nor did he ask personal questions about her studies or her family. When he dated someone, which wasn't often, Emily noted that he never seemed thoroughly engaged or delighted with her, and watched his short-lived girlfriends work like crazy to capture and hold his attention without success. Barrett was austere and focused, totally driven by business purposes. Further, he was reserved, old-school and buttoned-up, and in the twenty-four years Emily had known him, she couldn't ever remember seeing him let loose. It was like he was born with an expensive tie around his neck and a leather briefcase attached to his hand.

And yet . . .

His reserved manners didn't bother Emily; Barrett spoke with economy and precision which meant every word was well-placed and reliably exact in meaning. He was so smart it made her head spin, and so well-informed she wondered how he found the time to read so much. He was strong and powerful, and Emily marveled that he'd achieved so much and was so respected in his field by thirty-two years old. The way Barrett commanded a table made her feel safe with him—like nothing would dare bother her with Barrett's strong presence beside her—and she liked the way his business associates looked at her, like she must be something special to have wrangled the heart of Mr. English. Lately, in her more romantic daydreams, Emily imagined Barrett a modern-day Mr. Darcy to her bookish Elizabeth, wondering how deep his still waters ran and having a notion that needling him a little might rattle him from his austerity and cast more light on his character.

And the way he made her *feel* . . .

When Emily met Barrett for their dates, his eyes would flash with something indefinable but sharp, almost like pain or disapproval or *hunger*, which made her breath catch, because it meant that—on some level—she affected him. When he introduced her to his associates as his fiancée, it made her tremble, and she often had to steady her hand before offering it to his guests. At times she'd feel his glance linger on her profile as she sat beside him, and it made her skin flush and her heart race to feel his eyes focused so intently on her. Occasionally he'd place his hand on her lower back as he guided her to a table, or their fingers would touch as they reached for their wineglasses, and butterflies would mass and throng in her tummy. The way her name rumbled off his tongue: *Emily* . . . was so decadent and low and intimate in her ears, she had to work to keep her eyes from fluttering closed in pleasure as the muscles deep inside of her body clenched with urgency.

. . . isn't there anything you like about him?

How could she tell the truth? Even as a little girl, eight years his junior, she'd always liked Barrett the best, awed by his innate power and strength. But playing his fiancée with regularity over the past few months had ensured that her attraction to Barrett knew no bounds. It sat quietly in wait for Barrett to make a move—any move—that would allow her to hope that his heart could be moved by hers.

That was the biggest problem of all: even with her education and perfectly respectable upbringing, Emily was the help, the gardener's daughter, the housekeeper's little girl. She was ridiculous for thinking—for hoping, for wishing, even for a moment—she could ever be a fit match for the heart of Barrett English.

She flinched, discomfort and a rush of panic making her feel slightly breathless, as she forced herself to face the fact that what had always been a slow-burning infatuation had heated to a boiling point over the last few months. Indeed, if Emily was honest with herself she knew she'd fallen in love with Barrett, a circumstance which was entirely unacceptable and needed correction. Soon.

"Emily?" prompted Val. "*Anything?*"

Emily forced a deep breath, her heart heavy as she promised to examine her feelings more thoroughly later and decide, once and for all, what action they warranted.

"Well . . ." said Emily, trying to come up with something trite to appease Valeria's curiosity without betraying her true struggles. "He always remembers to order me a glass of Riesling."

"That's something, I guess," said Emily's roommate. She walked along in silence beside Emily for a few minutes as fall leaves swirled around their feet. "But wait. You only drink beer at home. Do you even *like* Riesling?"

"Not really."

Valeria glanced at Emily incredulously before her shoulders started trembling with laughter. "So the thing you like best about Barrett English is that he orders you the same drink every time, even though it happens to be a drink you don't even like?"

"I guess so," said Emily, giggling along with her friend, the silliness a reprieve from the hopelessness of her heart.

"That's pathetic Emily," said Valeria, unlocking the outside door to their walk-up. "But on the bright side, at least you'll make three to four hundred dollars for your time tomorrow. How about we splurge on Chinese tonight?"

"Chinese on Barrett English," said Emily, following her roommate up the stairs. "I like it. And let's eat it straight out of the containers. I bet Barrett's never done that in his whole master-of-the-universe life."

At that very moment Barrett English, so-called Master of the Universe, was a force to be reckoned with. He stared at two of his four younger brothers with one eyebrow raised and his hands tented under his chin.

"You can't do it," insisted Fitz, Chief Compliance Officer of English & Sons, looking to Alex for help.

"Fitz is right, Barrett. Harrison's going to dig in his heels."

When Barrett sat at his massive cherry desk on the nineteenth floor of the newest, trendiest, most expensive office building in Philadelphia, he didn't often take no for an answer. Frankly, Barrett rarely took no for an answer regardless of where he was sitting.

"You're going to need his cooperation," said Fitz, who had always been more of a rule-follower than Barrett, which Barrett both envied and considered a weakness. "You can't just bulldoze your way into the situation, threatening an acquisition of the largest shipbuilding company on the east coast. J.J. Harrison still owns thirty percent of the company, not to mention the employees love him like a father. You force him out, you risk the employees walking, and you'll be left with nothing but a shell of a company. You're going to have to win him over."

Alex looked at Barrett, then quirked his lips up, suppressing a grin at Fitz's impassioned plea. Alex was the most easygoing of the five brothers. Both in and out of the office he had a perpetual smirk on his face which made him the target of all women everywhere. Again, a quality Barrett was grudgingly envious of, even as he turned his nose up at Alex's shenanigans, which frequently caused uncomfortable romantic tangles for his middle brother. Barrett wasn't interested in any of that. He was Barrett English. He didn't have time for that sort of nonsense.

When he felt frustrated for female company, he called Felicity Atwell and they scratched each other's mutual itch in the suite of an expensive hotel before going their separate ways. He didn't require or desire more of an attachment than that.

Mostly.

He flicked his eyes down at his desk where he'd written a reminder to himself to call the sommelier at the Union League Club to ensure they had the Egon Müller Riesling icy cold and uncorked promptly at seven-o-five tomorrow night. There were twenty-four hours between now and then—they could have a bottle imported from Germany in that time, if needed. If Emily insisted on drinking that sweet slop, at least she should be drinking the best.

"I'm just saying, more bees with honey," said Fitz, looking a little desperately at Alex. "Maybe Alex or I should . . ."

Barrett saw the silent message pass between his younger brothers. They didn't think he could swing this deal because he wasn't charming enough? He suppressed a snort. Charm didn't get deals done. Strength and focus did.

"I'll handle it," replied Barrett tersely, sitting straight in his chair and picking up the receiver of his desk phone. "Anything else?"

Fitz shifted in the guest chair behind Barrett's desk, glancing at Alex again. "Do you have a . . . a date for tomorrow? It would help keep things friendly."

"Not that it's any of your business, Fitz, but I do."

Alex leaned forward. "But it's not Emily Edwards, is it?"

Barrett bristled, settling the phone slowly back into its cradle and staring at Alex with cold eyes. "Say what you want to say, Alex. I've got more important things to do."

Alex put his hands up. "Emily's a great girl. We all like Emily."

Fitz nodded carefully, his eyes direct and cool. "And we're all quite fond of Felix and Susannah, of course."

"Of course," agreed Alex.

"Of course," said Barrett, drily. He raised an eyebrow. "So . . . ?"

"You could bring Felicity Atwell or any of the other girls you met at Penn."

"Not interested. They'd read into it on a personal level. Could get messy."

"And Emily won't?" asked Fitz, something flickering behind his eyes. "Read into it? Get messy?"

Oh. Barrett understood. They were concerned Emily would form an attachment to him and she'd get hurt at some point, causing potential awkwardness with their beloved gardener and housekeeper. Well then, they underestimated Emily.

She may have started out as the gardener's daughter, but she'd attended U Penn, just like the English brothers. She was smart and beautiful and an even match for any of the girls Barrett had met at Penn. And okay, Emily might not have a trust fund, but when she dressed up like any other high society girl, laughing her soft, throaty chuckle at all of the appropriate times? He didn't care if her bank account was next to empty, and he couldn't give a crap that she grew up in the gatehouse. It was so damn distracting, he was almost grateful for her outstretched hand at the end of the night. It acted as a wake-up call, reminding him she had reluctantly agreed to work for him, and they *weren't* actually dating, no matter how much the fantasy had taken root in his heart.

Besides, he was eight years her senior. He remembered her in pigtails waiting for the school bus as he'd driven himself to college. And he was self-aware enough to note that while Fitz was full of heart and Alex was a veritable Casanova, Barrett was considered stuffy and reserved, while Emily was—as she had always been—young, bright-eyed, warm, and engaging.

Sitting beside her, he'd searched her face surreptitiously as the weeks slipped by, looking for any sign that she might be interested in him—that she saw beyond his stern manners and business dealings, that she could see him as someone other than the oldest English brother, or worse, "the Shark." Alas . . . Emily was polite and professional, on-time, accommodating of his schedule, and so breathtakingly beautiful, it made his heart hurt. But as far as he could tell, and regardless of the growing—and completely ridiculous—feelings he had for her, she gave no outward indication she was interested in him romantically. And anxious not to thrust the nature of his true feelings upon her, possibly risking the generations-old relationship his family had with hers, he remained silent.

"No," answered Barrett. "She won't read into it, and it won't get messy."

"Just don't crap where you eat, Barrett."

"Screw you, Alex. You're in no position to talk. How many girls have we had to quietly pay off now? And there was that charming situation with the video tape."

Alex flushed, but Barrett could tell it was less out of embarrassment than pride. Barrett rolled his eyes at his little brother.

"I'm all about business, boys. And I can guarantee you—without any shadow of doubt—that Emily's all about business too."

"Business?" asked Fitz, eyebrows furrowing, sensing some ethical quandary, no doubt.

"The Edwardses have always worked for the Englishes."

"So she's *working* for you?"

"She's not on the payroll," said Alex, their Chief Financial Officer.

"It's under control, Alex."

"Oh, I'll just bet it is," said Alex, giving up the argument. He stood and pushed his chair back under the lip of his oldest brother's desk, turning to leave.

Fitz hesitated, and Barrett could see the moral dilemma taking place in his brother's head. There was a reason Fitz was a natural at compliance. Following the rules was innate to him. Almost always.

"Fitz," said Barrett in a more gentle tone, mostly reserved for family gatherings and out-of-the-office social occasions. He leaned forward, capturing his brother's blue eyes, so much like his own. "There's nothing to worry about. I promise."

Fitz took a deep breath and surrendered, bracing his hands on the front of Barrett's desk to stand and follow Alex out of the room.

As soon as they were gone, Barrett swiveled in his chair, looking out over Philadelphia as he tightened his jaw then released it. It *was* under control, wasn't it? Of course it was, despite the fact that Barrett had been captivated by Emily Edwards for almost as long as he could remember.

He clearly remembered the day, twenty-four years ago, when Felix and Susannah had brought their newborn daughter up to the main house to meet the English family. She'd been this tiny perfect person with bright blue eyes and fuzzy light hair covering her otherwise bald head. Like most other eight-year-olds, Barrett wasn't very interested in babies, especially since there'd been a new English baby brother in his life every other year since he was born. But from the beginning, Emily was different.

First of all, she was the first baby *girl* he'd ever seen, and it surprised him how much more delicate and soft she looked. Weston and Emily were right around the same age, but Weston's face was always knitted intensely, as though he knew he'd have to fight for his place among four older siblings. Weston's bellow was loud and demanding, whereas baby Emily lay quietly in her mother's arms, wrapped up in a pale pink blanket, taking in the world with those cerulean eyes from the warmth of her snug nest.

Susannah, noticing his quiet interest in her daughter, had asked Barrett if he wanted to hold Emily. Barrett had nodded eagerly, sitting on the silk brocaded loveseat beside her. Susannah had gently transferred the little girl to Barrett's arms, and he'd stared down at her, dumbstruck, for several long moments as their parents visited. His father had even opened a bottle of champagne, and the four adults had toasted baby Emily while Barrett held her carefully, reverently, on his lap. Fitz and Alex wrestled in the corner, Stratton quietly looked at a picture book on the floor, and Weston—predictably—started bellowing from his cradle for attention. But, Barrett was in his own world where nothing else existed but the little girl in his arms, who locked her brand new blue eyes on his and held on.

"Ridiculous sentiment," he muttered, swiveling his chair back around and picking up the phone. "Get Lox and Ravers now. I want to go over the Harrison numbers once more before I leave today."

"It's seven o'clock, sir."

"I don't care if it's midnight. Get them here." He hung up the phone.

Barrett clenched his jaw, forcing her blue eyes out of his mind, as he'd done a million times before, and opened up a new spreadsheet. He'd learned long ago the only antidote to useless longing was hard work, and there was *always* more to do.

Chapter 2

Emily stood in front of her closet, staring at the two outfits Barrett had sent to her soon after she'd agreed to play fiancée for him several months ago: a Givenchy couture black, silk cocktail dress that cost more than two months' rent, and a light blue custom-made Chanel suit that cost *three times* more than two months' rent. It was hands down the most expensive thing in Emily's apartment.

She almost always chose to wear the black dress, mostly because the one time she'd worn the Chanel, Barrett's eyes had darkened appreciably like she'd done something wrong, which made no sense at all since he'd purchased the suit for her to wear in the first place. Honestly, she loved it. It hugged her size eight curves on top, but sucked her in at the waist and fell to a flattering but tasteful line across her thighs. Not to mention, the fabric color was such a close match to her eyes, it was almost unreal how blue they became when she wore it. But, he'd looked so displeased after the first time, she hadn't worn it again.

She huffed, taking the beautiful blue suit out of the closet, watching as the clear cellophane from the dry cleaners rustled lightly over it.

"I don't feel like black tonight. I'm wearing the suit, and I don't care if you like it or not, Barrett."

She pulled on her white cotton underwear and simple Playtex bra—it's not like she could afford La Perla to go underneath—and, keeping with the propriety of being Barrett English's fiancée, she pulled on some nude pantyhose with a scowl. A cream silk camisole covered her simple bra and tickled the skin of her stomach. Barrett had sent one pair of size seven black patent leather Coach pumps that were boring, but comfortable, and she slipped those over her feet, remembering the awkwardness of his proposition.

It was several months ago in late-spring, and Emily had been sitting on a bench outside of College Hall at the University of Pennsylvania, where she was a first-year doctoral student, when she heard him say her name.

"Emily Edwards?"

She looked up, shielding her eyes from the glare of the sun to see Barrett's handsome face come into focus. "Barrett?"

"Yes. Hello. I thought that was you. I was here for an endowment meeting. Decided to stroll the campus for a few minutes before heading back to the office."

Stroll the campus. She grinned up at him. Barrett English always spoke like someone much older than his thirty-two years, but she sort of liked that about him. It was part of who he was.

In contrast to his stiff conversation was the way he looked—easy, smooth, and ridiculously debonair. Her eyes flicked down for a second to check out the cut of his suit, which was obviously custom made, because it fit him like a dream. Navy blue and sharp, it was the perfect complement to the light blue dress shirt with bright white French cuffs underneath. Her eyes touched on his wrists where shiny silver cufflinks were engraved with *BEE.* Barrett Edward English. It was good the sun was so bright—he wasn't able to see her pupils dilate with a lifetime's worth of lust.

"I'm interrupting you," he observed.

"It's fine." Emily's eyes strained against the sun, narrowed to slits in an attempt to maintain eye contact. "Do, um, do you want to sit?"

"No. How are your parents?"

"Very well, thank you. And yours?"

"Fine."

"Fitz, Alex, Stratton, and Weston?"

"All well, thank you."

Her shoulders slumped in disappointment as their pleasantries found a dead end.

Why did she wish, every time she saw him, which wasn't very often, that he'd loosen up with her? It's not like she had a chance with him, so why did it matter? Maybe because they'd known one another forever, and yet, they didn't actually know one another very well at all. What was it about Barrett that had always made her heart thump faster and her eyes widen with longing? And what would it take to get Barrett to be even a little bit playful? Was it even possible?

The sun was so intense, Emily couldn't bear the glare anymore. She had looked down at the notes on her lap, blinking to clear her vision, hoping she didn't appear dismissive as her pulse pounded in her neck.

The silence had grown thick and awkward between them, and she finally wondered if he was waiting for her to politely say "good-bye," releasing him from her company.

"Well . . ." she had started. "It was nice of you to say hel—"

"Are you dating anyone?"

Taken off-guard, Emily had gasped, then scoffed lightly, looking back up to see if he was serious. Without a smile to soften the boldness of the question, it appeared as though he was. "W-What? Why are you asking?"

"I'm just wondering," he answered, his blue eyes boring into hers.

Her heart had surged behind her ribs, racing like a prizewinner at Preakness. "N-no. Not right now."

"Then I have a proposition for you." His voice was businesslike and level, but the word "proposition" hung between them, loaded and—she guessed unintentionally—suggestive.

"Oh?"

"I need a—well, what I need is a woman to occasionally—"

"Barrett!" she exclaimed, a flush starting at her breasts and creeping steadily up her neck to scorch her cheeks.

"No, no! Nothing like that. Don't be ludicrous, Emily," he said, quickly moving to sit beside her. His thigh pressed against hers, and if anything was ludicrous, it was the jolt she got from that tiny bit of contact. She turned to find him looking at her seriously, and he searched her eyes as he added, "I don't want any romantic complications."

Her jaw dropped, and her eyes widened with offense. "Now you listen to me, Barrett English. My family may work for yours, but I am *not* that kind of girl and you have no right suggesting that we—"

"No! Damn it. I said it wasn't like that. That's not—I mean, I need a date. Occasionally. I need a woman to pose as my fiancée from time to time."

She couldn't have been more shocked if he'd stripped out of his Armani suit and done the Macarena for her.

"Come again?"

He looked at his lap before seizing her eyes in the no-nonsense stare he must use for all of his corporate dealings, and she started to understand why his nickname was "the Shark." His gaze was focused and unyielding, she found it incredibly exciting.

"Emily, let me be quite clear. I am offering you a job. I would like to pay you to occasionally accompany me to business dinners posing as my fiancée. I will supply one ring, two dresses, and one pair of shoes so that you are appropriately attired for such engagements. I will always have a car pick you up and drop you off at your apartment so your safety will never be compromised. I will not require anything untoward whatsoever. I just want your occasional company for the sake of appearances. That's all."

"You want to pay me to go on business dates with you?"

He nodded. "As my fiancée."

Emily was so turned around by the course of their conversation, she took a brief glimpse over her shoulder to see if Alex English was hiding behind a tree, taping this exchange as some sort of family prank.

No Alex. Back to Barrett.

"Do you mind if I ask why?"

"I don't trust that many people, Emily, but I trust you."

She didn't want it to matter that he'd said that, but it did. It was a rare show of feeling from Barrett, she sensed, and the direct way he had said it made her heart lurch with hopefulness. She looked down at her lap, finding it easier to compose herself when she wasn't looking into his searing blue eyes.

"Don't you have a dozen women you could ask to do this? I mean, in *your* world?"

He shrugged beside her. "It could get messy. I don't want messy. I prefer neat."

And that lovely surge of happiness had evaporated into thin air. Of course. He was an English, and she was an Edwards, and he was merely hiring her to do a job. Further, he was basically saying he had no romantic interest in her and never would, so she was a perfect choice for non-messy, fake-fiancée employment.

Though Barrett had never been more than a far-reaching fantasy, it still hurt Emily's feelings a little that he should be so frank about how unappealing and unsuitable she was. She sensed he wasn't purposely trying to hurt her, but it did make her decision to refuse him easy, because she knew in her heart that even though she wouldn't be messy for *him*, he could be potentially messy for *her*.

"I don't think so, Barrett. I'm a first-year doctoral student. Even over the summer, I have to keep up with my studies. I tutor undergrads. I'm interning for one of the professors this summer. I don't, you know, I don't really date much. I'm working on my—"

"I'll pay you a hundred dollars an hour for your time."

Emily's jaw dropped as her lungs emptied like the wind had been knocked out of her. For a struggling student, that was an unthinkable amount of money for occasionally sitting next to him at dinner. She had stared at him for what seemed like an eternity before taking a deep breath and raising her hand to him. "Where and when?"

His lips twitched as he gave her a brief, inscrutable smile, then took her hand and shook it, causing a delicious current to trail from her palm to her wrist, up her arm and down her back, tripping the pulse in her neck.

"I'll be in touch," he had said, looking down at their clasped hands for a long moment before pulling his away.

Since then, Emily had been on seven dates as the future Mrs. Barrett English, always at the Union League Club, always with different business associates of Barrett's and always wearing the "engagement" ring Barrett had sent her via courier before their first date with the incredibly romantic note attached that read: *It's paste, but it's good paste. Don't lose it. —B*

Twisting her light blonde hair up into a chignon for date number eight, Emily looked at herself in the mirror. From the respectable distance of her station while growing up at Haverford Park, she'd had a front row seat to every English family soiree, every important social gathering at their Blueberry Lane estate, and a close-up look at every girlfriend brought home by the five handsome brothers.

Emily had learned how to dress, speak and act to fit in with the English family, who, when they encountered her, treated her like an almost-forgotten second or third cousin, of whom they were vaguely fond but unconcerned. Though she wasn't formally invited to any of their social events, with the exception of Boxing Day and the annual Summer Party, living on their property in close daily contact with the family had afforded Emily a certain education on how to fit in with the upper crust of posh Haverford. That was another reason that Barrett had chosen her to act as his fiancée: he knew she could pull it off.

Emily dusted some blush on her pale cheekbones and brushed some mascara on her light lashes, then swiped a bit of pale pink lip gloss across her lips. Subtle. Understated. Perfect. And all for him. Not that Barrett would notice or care.

As she pulled on the light blue tweed skirt, adjusting the gold link belt that accented her trim waist, she considered the question Valeria had asked yesterday and the very real feelings it had forced Emily to recognize.

Being "engaged" to Barrett wasn't just a job anymore. Emily loved being Barrett English's fake fiancée, which was not just inconvenient, but pointless. Because despite her deepening feelings, heart flutters, and silent longings, Barrett had made it clear from the start she held no romantic interest for him. Falling for Barrett was not only one-sided, but a recipe for heartbreak.

Emily looked at herself in the mirror, buttoning the mother-of-pearl buttons on the perfect-fitting cropped jacket, then running her hands slowly and regretfully over the beautiful material before grabbing her purse and heading for the door. She had looked at the situation from every angle, but regrettably had come up with only one feasible solution.

Before her feelings for Barrett developed any further, she needed to "break up" with him.

"Another day another dollar, eh, Smith?" said Emily, ducking under Smith's umbrella to take a seat in the back of the custom-fitted town car.

"If you can't beat 'em, join 'em, Miss Em," said Smith, taking his seat behind the wheel.

"Damned if you do and damned if you don't," she answered, cracking her window for fresh air as Smith pulled away from the curb in front of her apartment building.

"Don't bite the hand that feeds you, now."

Emily grinned. She'd been playing this game with the English family chauffeur, Reginald Smithson, since she was a very little girl when he used to call her "L'il Miss Em" and she'd occasionally help him wash the cars on the odd, lazy Sunday.

"Put your best foot forward."

"You win," said the older black man, chuckling and flicking his gaze up to Emily in the rearview mirror.

Emily leaned forward until her chin rested on the windowsill between the front and back seats of the luxury town car. "Still not mentioning these dates to Mom and Dad, right Smith?"

"I'm not one to stir up trouble, Miss Em, but I sure hope you know what you're doing."

"I promise you I do. You ever known me to act stupid?"

"Can't say I have, but there's a first for everything."

"Barrett's between girlfriends. He needs a date for these things, so I help out. That's all."

"*Between* girlfriends?" scoffed Smith. "That would require a girlfriend or two."

Emily sat back and asked as casually as possible, "Felicity Atwell?"

"She ain't no proper girlfriend, Miss Em. But that's all I'm gonna say about that. Mr. Barrett ain't had a *real* girlfriend in years, come to think of it. He has lady friends from time to time, but never someone special."

Emily sighed softly in relief. She knew every girl that every English boy had ever brought home, and Barrett hadn't brought home anyone special for a long time. Still, something inside of her relaxed knowing that Barrett's heart was free. *Not that it should matter to you at all*, she reminded herself, since she was determined to give him back the engagement ring tonight and tell him she wasn't available for any further dates.

"All work and no play makes Jack a dull boy," she said, ignoring the burn in the back of her eyes that declared how much she would miss seeing him.

"He got the skills to pay the bills."

"But he's got to be lonely," said Emily quietly.

"That ain't no cliché, child," said Smith. "But ain't it the truth."

Barrett held the umbrella over the car and reached for Emily's door so Smith wouldn't have to come out in the rain. Once she was safely beside him, he knocked on Smith's window, which lowered immediately.

"I'll call."

"That'd be fine, sir," answered Smith with a nod, pulling from the curb to find somewhere close by to park until he was needed.

With Emily so close to him under the umbrella, Barrett could smell her perfume. She had been wearing it since she was a teenager, which made it the most distracting scent ever created: Shalimar by Guerlain. The first bottle Emily ever received had actually been purchased by Barrett for his mother for Christmas, then re-gifted to Emily on Boxing Day when Eleanora English decided she didn't like the scent and realized she had forgotten to pick up a gift for the gardener's daughter. Emily had worn it ever since, which meant that as an adult she wore a perfume inadvertently chosen by Barrett.

"It's a dreadful evening," he muttered about the rain, putting his hand on the small of her back and ushering her into the club. He savored the brief bit of physical contact with her, reasoning that the sidewalks were slippery so the contact was necessary, not gratuitous, despite the way his body tightened.

"Who is it tonight?" she asked softly, pulling away the moment they were inside the vestibule of the club.

"Harrison Shipbuilding. J.J. Harrison and his wife, Hélène."

Her blue eyes turned to him in surprise. "His wife?"

Barrett had purposely omitted the fact that this dinner, unlike the others in which only other businesspeople were in attendance, would be more intimate and more social. "Yes."

She stared at him with thin lips and wide eyes, finally moving her hands to the knot at the waist of her black raincoat. He noticed every slight shift of her body, memorizing the spare grace of her movements, quietly marveling at them.

"We don't have our story ironed out enough to pass muster with a wife," she protested.

"What's the difference? J.J. and I are here to talk business."

"And I suppose Hélène and I should be mute?"

He shrugged. "It's not like you two are friends. Offer some small talk."

"Barrett! She's an older lady. They live for this stuff. She's going to ask about the wedding, our plans, how we met. That's what they do."

She turned, and he took the coat from her shoulders, suppressing a groan when he realized she'd chosen the blue suit. Damn it, why in the hell did he ever have it made for her in the first place if he couldn't bear to see her in it? He'd insisted the fabric match the blue of her eyes perfectly, but whenever she wore it, she was so breathtaking, it distracted him. He should have told her to wear the black instead.

She turned to face him and the hurt expression on her face clued him into the fact that he was glowering. He turned from her, handed the raincoat to the coat check girl, and then offered the claim ticket to Emily without a word.

He gestured toward the dining room, but she remained rooted, eyes large and annoyed.

"Our story?"

"Tell her whatever you want," he snapped, frustrated for wanting what he couldn't have. "I'll go along with it."

"Anything?" she asked with a hint of challenge in her voice.

"Within reason."

Her lips parted, and his eyes darted to them. He forced himself not to linger, cutting to her gaze again instead—to the same eyes that always dismissed him at the end of the night after he handed over the money she'd earned.

"I really don't care," he added. "As long as it's appropriate and plausible."

Her glossy, pink bottom lip slipped between her teeth for a moment. He hated it when she did that. Hours later, at home in his penthouse, it would take several scotches to forget what she looked like biting on that lip—how it made his blood rush south like a teenager in love.

"Appropriate and plausible. How romantic."

He took a deep breath and sighed. Was it his imagination or was she being more contrary than usual tonight?

He glanced at his watch. The Harrisons would be here in twenty minutes. Twenty minutes alone with Emily Edwards. One thousand, two hundred seconds of Emily all to himself.

"May I buy you a drink while we wait?"

Her lips were still pursed and sour as she turned toward the lounge area, leaving him to follow in her wake.

Chapter 3

"Oh, my dear!" exclaimed Hélène Harrison. "What a charming beginning! Simply *charmant*!"

Emily had just told Hélène that she and Barrett had grown up on the same road, a stone's throw away from each other, and yet they'd never dated until this past year when they ran into one another at Penn. Emily smiled politely, sipping her Riesling, feeling pleased with herself, then hiding a cringe at the sticky sweetness of the wine.

Why hadn't she told him she preferred a good microbrew beer over wine? The only time she'd ever drunk Riesling was the summer her cousin Daisy had visited. Fitz English, in a gesture totally and completely out of character, had stolen three bottles from his father's wine cellar in an effort to impress Daisy. Along with Alex and Weston, the five of them had gotten drunk as skunks on the trampoline near the pool, much to the disapproval of Barrett who came out around midnight and told them to keep it down or they were going to wake up the whole neighborhood. Emily barely recalled the walk back to the gatehouse at two o'clock in the morning, and had nursed a killer hangover the next morning. No doubt Barrett remembered as well, forcing her to drink the sweet, syrupy stuff as a reminder of the night she got soused, and a precautionary measure against further untoward behavior.

She glanced over at him, deeply engaged in conversation with J.J. Harrison who had his arms crossed over his chest, looking at Barrett with something that strongly resembled distaste. Despite the care she'd taken getting ready tonight, Barrett had grimaced when she took off her raincoat, and it had hurt her feelings. They'd headed over to the bar and sat in veritable silence side-by-side until the Harrisons had arrived, and after introducing Emily as his fiancée, he'd barely glanced her way again.

Her hurt feelings coupled with the fact that Emily was breaking off their fake engagement at the end of the night, made her uncharacteristically reckless. She vaguely considered her Darcy-Elizabeth theory and wondered what reaction a little needling of Barrett would produce. Warming to the idea quickly and ignoring the warning bells going off in her head, she formulated a quick plan: Operation Poke the Shark.

Downing her entire glass of wine in one gulp and flashing her most brilliant smile, Emily gestured for the older woman to lean closer in confidence. "Hélène, that's only how we *met*. There's so much more to the story."

Emily swallowed nervously, hiding it by keeping her smile plastered to her face. She looked over at Barrett, who continued to talk business, and although she knew it wasn't professional and she knew Operation Poke the Shark could (and likely *would*) backfire, leaving her humiliated, a lifetime's worth of longing wouldn't be denied. She'd never be this close to Barrett again after tonight, never have this sort of access to him. It was her last chance to figure out who Barrett was and if her hunches about him were founded in anything besides a lifelong infatuation, and completely one-sided. Despite the potential for awkwardness between them, she simply couldn't let this one-time opportunity slip through her fingers.

Taking a deep breath, she summoned her courage and stared at Barrett's hand for a long moment before reaching for it with trembling fingers and raising it to her lips.

Distracted by the scent of soap and starch, she lingered over the warm skin on the back of his hand, letting her lips drag softly together to meet in a soft kiss. Barrett's low baritone ceased abruptly and when Emily looked up, he'd turned his attention completely to her. His eyes were wide, deep and dark, anchored somewhere between shocked and furious.

Almost void of bravery, she mustered her last bit of spirit and gave him the sexiest grin she could manage, while keeping her voice from wavering. "Shall I tell it, darling, or will you?"

"W-what? Tell wh—Emily, what are you talking about?"

"Our story, Barrett," she insisted, brushing his skin with her lips again as her stomach flip-flopped not only from her reckless daring, but from the contact—from the heat rising from his hand, warming her lips.

His nostrils flared and his eyes narrowed. "I'm sure our guests—"

"Want to hear every word!" exclaimed Hélène, finishing off her second gin and tonic and leaning forward excitedly. "Two such attractive people so obviously in love."

"Hear that, darling?" asked Emily, amazed that she hadn't backed down from his scowl yet. She laced her fingers through his before setting their joined hands on the table.

He stared at her in disbelief, his breathing noticeably shallow. "I, um, I—"

Feeling marginally more confident at the doorstep of a flummoxed Barrett, Emily grinned at Hélène. "Barrett's a tiger in the boardroom, but a lamb in the . . ."

Hélène's eyes widened, and for a moment Emily wondered if Barrett would break her fingers, he gripped them so tightly. She looked down at his white knuckles and concealed a pained grimace with her brightest possible smile.

". . . jewelry store."

"Oh!" said Hélène, her eyes flicking to the large, high-quality fake diamond on Emily's finger. "You're *wicked*, Emily!"

"I'd like to hear more about the softer side of Barrett English," said J.J. Harrison, relaxing for the first time all evening as he put his arm around Hélène and beckoned the waiter over to serve another round of drinks.

"J.J.," said Barrett in a strangled voice, "we could let the ladies chit-chat and retire to the bar to finalize—"

"Nonsense," said J.J., finishing the rest of his scotch. "Tell us all about Barrett, Emily. How the shark won the fair maiden's heart."

"Well, Barrett a—and, um . . ." started Emily, then sputtered, distracted by an unexpected, new development. Barrett's fingers loosened as his thumb started idly stroking the skin of Emily's hand. She glanced down, caught totally off-guard by the small movement, even a little bewildered. It was so slight, so subtle, but it felt so . . . *intimate* that her breath hitched. She flicked her gaze up to Barrett's face. His eyes were as dark as a stormy sea, focused on hers with searing intensity. Oh, Lord, he was furious with her. Furious? Or something else altogether? She wondered with a growing awareness that spread through her gut like molten lava—

"Emily?" he prompted, his voice softer and lower than she could ever remember hearing it. "Our story?"

"I . . ." she started, but her voice faltered, and he raised an eyebrow as the tables turned, seeming to enjoy her sudden discomfiture. Glancing down at their hands, his lips tilted up in a knowing smirk, and his eyes, which told her he had finally surrendered to her little game, took on the steely glint of challenge.

"Tell them, Emily. Tell them how I asked you. Tell them what I said when I asked you to be my wife."

His thumb still stroked softly, and his fingers flexed to grip hers closer, making her heart race painfully. His eyes were dark and intense, focused completely on her like a predator sizing up its prey for dinner. She swallowed the growing lump in her throat; she'd never had Barrett's focused attention quite like this. She felt the heat of his gaze in every fiber of her being.

"Emily?" prompted Hélène.

Emily plastered a smile on her face and turned to the older woman. "It was a Sunday," said Emily softly.

"A Sunday morning, *darling*," added Barrett.

Emily's breath caught. She was deeply aroused by Barrett's touch, by the low, provocative tone in his voice when he called her "darling." She'd never, ever seen this side of him. The moment she'd pressed her lips to his hand, a flip had switched, charging the very air between them, changing the rules they'd been following for the past few months. Operation Poke the Shark was up and running it seemed, and Emily knew enough of his fiercely competitive business nature to know that if she was going to bait him, he'd not only take the bait, he'd devour her too. If she was honest, it's exactly what she'd wanted—to force her Mr. Darcy to show her some emotion.

The Harrisons stared at her, eagerly awaiting her story. She swallowed, desperately trying to ignore the way Barrett's thumb was making her so hot she could barely focus.

Think, think, think. An engagement story. Think, Emily!

"Um. Well. We'd decided to visit the Japanese House and Garden, b-because Barrett had never seen it."

"You're skipping so much, Emily," he scolded, lifting their hands and letting his lips linger on the back of her hand just as she'd done to him a few minutes ago. She concealed a gasp by reaching for her full wineglass, the muscles inside her body rousing themselves, flexing from the erotic sensation of his lips on her skin. She perceived the low rumble of a chuckle against her hand before he continued in a low, taut voice. "It was one of those lazy mornings when you wake up late because you have nowhere to be. Nowhere else you *want* to be."

His tone was so smooth, so suggestive, for a moment she almost felt like she could search her brain to actually find the memory of waking up beside him, his naked chest pressed up against her back as the light filtered in through his bedroom. She'd never been in Barrett's bedroom, but she imagined it was impersonal and perfectly appointed with a massive bed and crisp white sheets.

Something about envisioning his cold, austere bedroom gave her a jolt of spirit, and after a healthy gulp, she placed her glass back down on the table, turning to him to lick her lower lip before biting down on it slowly.

"You made me brunch, Bee," she purred, letting the fantasy embolden her.

His eyes widened slightly at the nickname before he turned to the Harrisons who were wide-eyed, focused on every word. In a theatrical whisper that made Emily's lips quirk up at the same time her toes curled, Barrett confided, "She is *insatiable* in the morning."

"Oh!" sighed Hélène, fanning herself. "Oh my!"

"Now who's wicked?" asked Emily, her eyes widening at his unexpected innuendo. She uncrossed her legs under the table and shifted just slightly to press her thigh up against Barrett's. She watched his nostrils flair and she grinned at him with satisfaction. "After brunch—"

"What does an English make for brunch?" interrupted J.J., a curious smile playing on his face.

"Blueberry pancakes," blurted out Barrett, and Emily chuckled softly looking up at him with surprised eyes.

Blueberry pancakes were her favorite.

At first, Barrett had been furious with her for pulling a stunt like this. He swore he wouldn't pay her a dime for tonight's debacle, as he tried to redirect the conversation back to business. He'd been making progress with J.J., his light threats doing their work on his quarry's head. But then her lips had touched his hand, shooting a direct line of heat to his groin, and he was—for the first time he could remember—so distracted by something other than business, he'd almost been speechless.

She'd caught him totally off-guard with her antics, and as much as propriety ranked high on Barrett's list of musts, it had taken him several serious minutes to talk himself out of hauling her out of her chair, thrusting his hand into her silky blonde hair and forcing his tongue into her mouth. By the time he'd gotten himself under control, there was no turning back. The Harrisons wanted a story.

But, two could play her game, and it wasn't lost on him when she started stuttering, her bravado faltering as he rubbed slow circles in the soft skin of her hand. He'd smirked at her then, relieved that if they were going to play, the field was at least level.

Just now, her bright blue eyes had lost the artifice of their shenanigans for a moment when he mentioned blueberry pancakes. They were her favorite, and he had no idea how he knew that, but he did.

Likely, he'd watched surreptitiously some time or another when she chose them at the Boxing Day buffet, or overheard Susannah remind Felix to get the ingredients for her birthday breakfast. He'd catalogued it in the corner of his mind reserved for Emily.

He shrugged. "They're your favorite."

"Yes, they are."

He pushed his leg meaningfully into hers, fully aware that she'd uncrossed her legs and her thighs were lightly spread, confined only by the narrow lines of her blue tweed skirt. He sipped his scotch then dropped his unoccupied hand to his lap, wondering what she would do if he slid it over, slipping it onto the warm skin of her thigh.

"And after pancakes?" prompted Hélène.

"Barrett doesn't dress like this on the weekends," said Emily, turning up her nose a little. *Hmm. She doesn't like the way I dress for business?* Something else to catalogue in the "Emily Corner." "He just wears jeans and a shirt. He walks around his apartment barefooted."

"Like a Polo model," said Hélène, fawning a little.

Barrett felt a flush of heat in his cheeks. He knew he was good-looking. He certainly used it to his advantage now and then, but he hated when it upstaged business dealings. Surprisingly, Emily chose that very moment to squeeze his hand lightly, as if she knew it bothered him.

"Naw. He's just Barrett. Barefoot in the kitchen making blueberry pancakes for his lazy fiancée."

He had a sudden image of her lazy in his bed, her blonde hair spread out on the white pillowcase, her eyes closed, her breasts peaked under a thin white sheet. He'd lower his head and capture one in his mouth, wetting the sheet around it to transparency as he sucked it into a tight point, before attending its twin. She'd wake up to his mouth, hot and wet, caressing her, and wind her fingers through his hair. Then he'd shove the sheet down so there was no barrier between his tongue and her sensitive nipples—

"What then?" asked Hélène eagerly.

"Emily, tell them the rest," he rasped, unable to escape from the fantasy playing in his head. He was utterly captivated by the story they were weaving of a happy young couple waking up to hot sex, pancakes, jeans, bare feet . . . it was like walking into a dream you'd been longing for, hoping for, wishing for your entire life. Although Barrett was working like hell to conceal it, he was as rapt as Hélène and J.J., wondering what happened next.

"I did the dishes because it's only fair to take care of him after he's taken care of me," she said softly, turning her luminous face to look up at him.

The words "take care of him" made another bolt of heat shoot down to his already growing erection, which tented his Armani suit pants under the table. He let his mind wander back to his fantasy of Emily in his bed, his lips skimming from her breasts to the flat, soft planes of her stomach, over a neat triangle of curls to the hidden bud of her throbbing sex that he'd take between his lips as he had her nipples, listening for her moans and whimpers as her fingers curled into the sheets by his head.

"Barrett?" asked Emily softly from beside him, still holding his eyes with hers.

Barrett swallowed deliberately, reaching for his scotch and dropping her eyes. He didn't want her to see the raw lust there, the lifetime of want. "Go on."

"Barrett was cagey when I came out from the bedroom all dressed. I suspected something was up."

He looked at her grin and sparkling blue eyes. "You were wearing that pink top with the pink sweater."

She nodded with surprise. It was the same outfit she'd been wearing when he "accidentally" bumped into her at Penn at few months ago.

"Barrett's lived in Philly all his life, and yet he'd never seen the Japanese House," said Emily softly.

"It takes a woman to make sure we get our dose of culture," said J.J. warmly, squeezing Hélène's shoulder affectionately.

Barrett turned his eyes back to Emily, realizing that for the first time—in a long, long time—he was actually having fun. And it felt good. Really good. "Emily's always been fascinated by history. Did you know she's a doctoral student at Penn?"

"Japanese studies?" asked Hélène.

"Early American," answered Emily, and her thumb lightly stroked the skin of his hand as he'd done to her before.

He swallowed, glancing down at their hands, and trying to keep the thread of conversation. Had such light contact been this distracting for her a few minutes ago? He recalled her stammer. He was affecting her just as much as she was him. It was a heady notion that cool as ice Emily Edwards was affected by him—he'd barely dared to hope she could ever see him as someone other than Barrett "the Shark" English, and now here she was beside him, spinning delicious tales and undamming a lifetime's worth of yearning for her. He didn't know what to do with this new information—not immediately—but it was firmly in the column of things he needed to explore further, in depth, after tonight.

"So you headed for the Japanese House . . ." said J.J., taking a slice of bread from the basket on the table and buttering it.

"Yes," Emily said, increasing the pressure against Barrett's thigh and making him grit his teeth.

He took the cue and picked up the story. "And what Emily didn't know, was that I'd visited the Japanese House the week before and arranged to have it all to ourselves for the afternoon."

Her thumb was still making mesmerizing circles on his skin.

"I couldn't figure out why it was so empty at first," she said, grinning up at him.

He smiled back, and it felt odd at first because he wasn't accustomed to smiling; smirking or polite half-grins were more his style.

"She called it a 'blue-sky-day' and kept berating the good citizens of Philadelphia for not appreciating a cultural treasure on such a beautiful day."

She chuckled lightly. "The garden is very lovely, Hélène, with flowering trees in whites and reds. And there are koi fish in a rock pond. We strolled over bridges and all the while I thought Barrett was indulging me, wishing he was back at home in his office closing on a big deal."

Is that really what she thought? That he'd rather be closing on a deal than spending time with her? He mulled her comment for a moment. She was right, of course. Even tonight, he'd been very annoyed when she'd started this whole engagement fantasy, but it shocked him to realize he hadn't actually turned his mind to business for a whole fifteen minutes now, distracted by Emily's body, captivated with the story they were creating.

"I assure you," he said quietly and firmly, lifting her hand to his lips again as his eyes seized hers hungrily. "When I have you all to myself, the last thing I'll be thinking about is business."

"*Mon Dieu!*" exclaimed Hélène, fanning her face again. "How romantic."

Emily's lips parted softly, her eyes losing some of their confidence to vulnerability. Her eyebrows furrowed ever so subtly. If he'd been looking any less intensely, he would have missed it.

"Barrett . . ." she whispered, searching his eyes with hers for a deeply intimate moment, and he felt the lines between game and reality, fiction and truth, blur irreparably. His heart raced and he thought about pulling her away from the table, finding a dark nook somewhere, and kissing her slowly and deeply without stopping for a long, long time. Would she let him? Was this game her way of telling him she'd fantasized about him the way he had about her?

"Emily sometimes forgets the romantic hidden deep inside of me."

"I do," she murmured in a daze, her eyes soft and supple, staring at him in languid fascination.

"But I had a lunch arranged at a small table under a cherry blossom tree."

"You did?" Her voice tilted up and his eyes widened at her, squeezing her hand a little harder, forcing her to shake herself out of her reverie, and play along. "You did," she said with more confidence. "A lunch. Under a cherry tree."

"And then he just . . . popped the question?" asked Hélène.

Barrett turned away from Emily, forcing a light smile for Hélène's benefit. "Not yet."

"We had lunch first," Emily said. "After lunch we gazed out at the gardens, and finally I said it was time to go."

"But I said it wasn't time to go. I dropped to one knee."

"And you asked me to be your wife."

"And you said yes."

Emily picked up her wineglass and downed the entire thing in a single gulp. "And I said yes."

Hélène and J.J. clapped quietly, offering their half-empty glasses for a toast and exclaiming over the romance of Barrett and Emily's love story.

Barrett flashed his eyes at J.J., feeling like the king of the world with Emily Edwards still holding his hand beside him. "You see, J.J.? I always get what I want in the end."

"We'll see, Shark," said J.J., his eyes narrowing. "We'll see about that."

Emily pulled her hand away from him to pick up her wineglass and he instantly missed the warmth of her fingers entwined with his. He pushed his thigh into hers, but she moved away slightly, crossing her leg to the other side. What had just happened? What had he missed?

When Barrett looked at Emily, her face was reserved and polite, as it always was at these dinners, and she smiled appropriately at him, then at the Harrisons, before excusing herself in a perfectly modulated voice to go to the ladies' room.

Chapter 4

Another cliché that Emily was particularly fond of? "Can't pull the wool over *her* eyes." And yet, she'd willfully pulled the wool over her own.

Emily sat on a puffy, mint green ottoman set in front of a low mirror and opened her small purse to root around for her lip gloss.

At first, she'd wanted see what would happen if she tried to rouse a little emotion in Barrett, but she'd never expected him to engage with her so playfully, eliciting emotions she had no business feeling. At the time, she'd wavered between enjoying the fun of it—the teasing and the flirtation, the surprising way he remembered her favorite breakfast food and spoke admiringly about her studies—and fantasizing that it was true, breathless with the way Barrett was making her feel. It was when he said, *"You see, J.J.? I always get what I want in the end,"* that everything had suddenly changed on a dime.

In that moment, Emily had reminded herself that she was doing a job and their night would end with three hundred dollars tidily transferred from his hands to hers. Barrett had never misrepresented himself. He'd made it clear from the start he had no romantic interest in her. She was an Edwards and he wasn't interested in messy romantic entanglements, so he'd drawn the lines boldly, placing employment and money between them.

And yet she *had* fallen for him, engaging in a dangerous fantasy that meant something real to her, that she would play out in her mind long after tonight. And the thought that it probably meant nothing to Barrett made her heart ache.

It was the words, *"When I have you all to myself, the last thing I'll be thinking about is business,"* that had made her heart soar to unsafe heights. As she'd gazed into his eyes, for the first time she could ever remember, his eyes weren't dark with anger or cool with indifference—they were hungry, but soft. Almost . . . tender. And while she couldn't ever *remember* seeing that expression in Barrett's eyes, she recognized it which meant she *had* seen it before. Deep, deep inside of her heart, on a visceral, primitive level, she knew he had looked at her with unmasked tenderness on one previous occasion of her life. Once before, he gazed at her like they were in a bubble together, like she was the sun and the moon and all of the stars—if not, how else would she have recognized it? Emily couldn't remember where or when, but she knew it was true and it made her stupid heart leap with hope.

Stupid because Barrett English was playing a little game with her for the sake of Hélène and J.J. Harrison's amusement. A game. Nothing more. After that performance, no doubt the business deal would be sealed upon her return to the table. Then he would call Smith to pick her up, slip the money inconspicuously into her palm as they shook hands good-night, and she wouldn't see him again until she was needed.

She stared at herself in the mirror, more determined than ever to let go of this charade. Whatever she felt in her head for Barrett before tonight's dinner had become significantly more substantial in her heart over the last half hour, and she needed to place distance between them. Now. Immediately. No matter what, she needed to break up with him so she could begin the painful process of getting over him.

She was distracted by the faint ringing of her phone in her bag and replaced the top of her lip gloss, throwing it back in her purse and fishing her phone out.

Her parent's number. At nine o'clock on a Friday night. She creased her brows. It wasn't the typical time she'd expect a call from them.

"Mom?"

"Emmy," her father's tone was serious, but sounded relieved to hear her voice.

"Is everything okay, Dad?"

"Now, I don't want you to worry, honey."

Emily's blood rushed cold as her fingers tightened on the phone. She was the only child of her aging parents. Their "little miracle," Emily had blessed their lives when her parents had long given up hope of having a child of their own.

"What's happened?"

"It's your mother. She, um, she took a spill."

Emily stood up, pulling the drawstring on her purse and heading toward the ladies' room door. She needed to find a taxi and head out to Haverford. Now.

"What do you mean?"

"She fainted at the top of the grand staircase, Emmy. She took a bad fall."

The grand staircase was the massive marble staircase in the front foyer of the English house that split at a landing, branching off to the two wings of the second floor gallery where there were guest rooms, a library, and several other common rooms. The family's bedrooms were on the third floor, offering the best views of the estate.

"From the landing or the top?"

"She was found on the landing."

"Is she conscious, Dad?"

"In and out. She has a concussion."

"Where are you?"

"Over at Kindred Hospital."

"I'm leaving right now. I'm downtown, but I'll be there in forty-five minutes."

"Don't rush, Emmy. She's sleeping. I just . . . well, I got a little scared, because Susannah, well . . ." He choked up, and it twisted Emily's heart.

"It's okay, Dad. She's going to be okay. I'm on my way."

Emily burst out of the ladies' room, heading for the coat check, only belatedly remembering that she should quickly say good night to Barrett and the Harrisons. She approached the table, Barrett's eyes locking on hers, his brows creasing as she got closer. He and J.J. stood up politely as she reached the table.

"I'm so sorry to cut our evening short, but I just received an important phone call. I'm afraid I need to go immediately."

"What?" exclaimed Barrett. "Why? Where do you have to go?"

Emily swallowed, not trusting herself to share the news of her mother's accident, worried out of her mind.

"I have to go," she repeated, leaning down to brush her cheek against Hélène Harrison's. "It was so lovely meeting you."

"I hope we meet again soon. I was just telling Barrett that we're—"

"Thank you so much," managed Emily, swallowing the lump in her throat and turning away from the table to beeline for the coat check.

In her haste to find the ticket, or because of her shaking hands, her purse dropped to the floor, causing her credit card, a few dollars, her lip gloss, ID and apartment keys to scatter on the runner in front of the coat check window. She squeezed her eyes shut against the burn of tears, about to fall to her knees when she felt a strong hand on her shoulder.

"I'll get it."

She looked down at Barrett's dirty blond head. He squatted on the floor, gathering her things together, then reached up with the claim ticket which she handed to the coat check girl.

When he returned her purse, his eyes searched hers. "I'm sorry things got a little, um—you don't have to go, Emily. It was all just silliness."

She stared at him, slack-jawed, and it took her a full minute to realize what he was talking about. Oh, God. He meant their little game at the table. He thought she was leaving because of that?

"Barrett," she said, taking her coat from the coat check girl and shrugging into it as Barrett held the shoulders for her. "My mother fell down the stairs at Haverford Park. She's at Kindred. I need to get a cab."

His face changed in an instant, the elegant lines transforming effortlessly from emotion to business. He took his phone out of his pocket and pressed a button. "Smith? Car. Now. Front entrance. Emily needs to go to Kindred Hospital." His face was hard and his lips were tight as he stared at her. "I'm coming with you. Just let me explain to the Harrisons."

Emily shook her head, moving quickly toward the revolving door that led to the street. "No, Barrett. Don't leave your meeting. I messed it up enough for you tonight."

"You all but clinched the deal." He turned on his heel, looking back once to growl, "Don't leave. Wait for me, Emily."

Emily stood under the awning outside of the Union League Club, waiting for Smith to pull up and Barrett to join her, wondering what had caused her mother to fall. Had she been carrying something heavy and slipped or was it something more serious encroaching on her mother's health and stealing her balance? Emily's fingers were cold and she pumped them, wishing she'd brought gloves. An instant later Smith arrived, and Emily suddenly felt the comforting strength of Barrett's hand on the small of her back as he led her to the car and pulled the door shut behind them.

Barrett looked over at Emily, shadowed in the dim light of the backseat. He hadn't been alone with her in a car for a long time. Not since he was twenty and she was twelve, and he found her walking into town on a Saturday afternoon to pick up a few groceries for her mother. He'd pulled over and offered her a lift and though she'd seemed surprised at first, she'd opened the door and let him drive her to the store. Even though he had a pool party to attend in the neighboring town, he'd strolled the aisles with her, asking her about school, smiling when she called herself a "history dork." Half an hour later, he'd driven her home and Susannah had invited him to stay for hamburgers and hot dogs. He'd accepted the invitation, marveling at their use of paper plates and enjoying Susannah's excellent potato salad. Hours later, as they toasted s'mores with Felix and watched the fireflies, he'd remembered the pool party, which was long over by then.

Felix and Susannah had been an important part of Barrett's childhood and adolescence. He never remembered a day of his life when they weren't somewhere on the grounds of his parents' estate tending the gardens, fixing one of the fountains, serving at an elegant dinner or hustling up the stairs with a pile of fresh towels. Haverford Park, his parents' thirty-acre, ten-bedroom estate in tony Haverford, had more staff than Felix and Susannah, of course, but there was something special about the Edwards, and all of the English children knew it.

Emily's great-grandfather, Stuart Edwards, had been the gardener for Barrett's great-grandfather back in the 1920s, brought along from Canada when the English family first emigrated to Philadelphia. Her grandfather had taken over the position in the 1950s and her father had stepped up in the 1980s. For as long as the English family had lived at Haverford Park, the Edwards family had lived there too.

Except for Boxing Day, which the Englishes and Edwardses celebrated together every year, the annual Summer Party, to which the Edwards were always invited, and very occasional impromptu gatherings—like Barrett staying for hamburgers and hot dogs on an odd Saturday afternoon after helping Emily run an errand to the store—the two families didn't socialize, but co-existed peacefully, respecting the differences in their incomes and stations.

But for Barrett, Felix Edwards was more than just the third generation of Edwards men who had tended the gardens at Haverford Park. He and Susannah—and Emily, for that matter—had provided a sense of quiet stability at Haverford Park while Barrett's parents attended a multitude of business and social engagements throughout Barrett's childhood. Susannah often minded the five English brothers when his parents went out for the evening, telling them bedtime stories over hot cocoa and kissing them all good-night. She would tousle Barrett's hair affectionately when the five boys waited for the Catholic school bus that picked them up outside the gatehouse every weekday morning. Felix fixed up many a skinned knee with the Band-Aids he kept in the greenhouse. There was something terribly comforting about the constant presence of the Edwards family at Haverford Park, and Barrett was genuinely concerned about Emily's mother.

People didn't just fall down stairs. It was a symptom of something. Sitting beside Emily as the town car moved swiftly toward Haverford, Barrett took his phone out of his pocket and dialed a number.

"Victoria? Barrett English here. Yes, of course. Tell him we'll set something up next week. I need a favor."

He glanced over to see Emily still looking out the window despondently, the streetlights highlighting her worried features as they made good time leaving the city.

"You're still on the board at Kindred Hospital, I presume? Who's the best neurologist there?"

Emily's back straightened, and her neck turned slowly to look at him, her expression unreadable.

"I need you to call him. Tonight. Yes, now, I'm afraid. If he's not on duty, I need him to get dressed and head over there anyway. Yes. I need him to check on an important friend of our family, Susannah Edwards. Right."

He stared at Emily, watching her eyes suddenly glisten with tears as he listened to Victoria yammer on about improvements needed at the hospital.

"Are you still having the Harvest Ball in November? Yes. I'll buy a table. All right. Make it two. Yes, ten thousand for each is fine. Send the paperwork to Colleen on Monday."

Emily's lip quivered and she bit down on it to keep herself from crying. She looked so undone, he couldn't have torn his eyes away from her if he tried.

"I want a complete work up on Susannah Edwards, Victoria. Very good. Yes. Good night."

He tucked the phone into his breast pocket, keeping his face impassive as he gazed at Emily. He didn't know what he expected, but when she launched herself across the seat and into his arms, his heart had never felt so full.

When Emily began her night, she certainly didn't have the slightest intention of ending it tucked against the expensive cotton of Barrett's shirt, ruining it with tears as she sobbed uncontrollably. He didn't complain or say a word. He was speechless and still for a moment, probably processing the fact that she'd hurled herself at him, before pulling her into his arms and resting his chin on top of her head. After several minutes of sobs, she took a ragged breath and sniffled. That was when she realized how deeply inappropriate it was that she was practically sitting on top of Barrett, ensconced in his arms. And she knew she should pull away, but to save her life, she couldn't make herself move.

"I'm s-sorry, Barrett," she said softly, sniffling again and clearing her throat. "I'm just so w-worried."

His hand stroked her back lightly, his strong arms comforting as they held her tightly against him. "Victoria Lawson says Dr. Knightly is the best neurologist in Philly. I'm sure he'll get there before us. Try not to worry until you know what's going on."

"She's not young anymore," said Emily, thinking of her sixty-three-year-old mother's white temples and wrinkled cheek.

"Susannah?" He scoffed. "She'll always be young."

Emily leaned back, looking up at Barrett, who offered her a rare, genuine smile, small though it was.

"Who are you?" she murmured.

"Barrett English," he whispered.

"No." She shook her head slowly, searching his eyes in the dim light, aware that with every breath her breasts heaved into the hardness of his chest. "Barrett English is a shark."

"He's also a man."

Emily straightened a little in his arms, reaching up to trace the line of his cheekbone with her cold fingers. He flinched and his eyes closed for a brief moment as he clenched his jaw, otherwise remaining totally and completely still.

"I'm so worried," said Emily, palming his cheek and lifting her eyes to his. "Distract me, Barrett. Please."

His eyes widened for just a moment before he dropped his forehead to hers. His breath was hot on her lips and she barely had a moment to react before he reached for her hips and transferred her completely onto his lap so that she straddled him, her knees digging into the soft leather seat on either side of his thighs, which were gripped tightly between hers since her skirt was so narrow. She took a deep, gasping breath as he pulled her closer. Her breasts were flush against his chest, and she felt the fierce pounding of his heart between the layers of shirt and tweed, silk, and cotton.

"You sure you want this?" he groaned against her lips, his nose nuzzling hers.

"Right now, I *need* this," she answered.

He held her face, sinking his fingers into her hair as his eyes closed. He leaned forward to seal his soft, warm lips firmly over hers in the semi-darkness. His other hand slid over her hip to the side of her thigh, which he held in place, keeping her tightly nestled against the hardness of his sex. He kissed her upper lip lightly, nipping and teasing as she adjusted to the feel of him, the nearness of him. Grabbing her lower lip with his teeth, he gently nibbled on it too, his tongue lightly swiping across it, making her frustrated and needy. She wanted more. Oh my God, in her whole life she'd never wanted anything more.

Emily whimpered softly, the sound coming from the very back of her throat, as his mouth widened and his tongue parted the seam of her lips. He tasted like scotch and warmth, his tongue satiny smooth against hers as he tasted her for the first time too. He readjusted his head, tilting it in the other direction, then sucked her tongue into his mouth, eliciting a surprised moan from her. Heat shot from her mouth to her stomach, spreading there, making her panties damp as she clenched muscles deep inside that had almost forgotten what it felt like for a kiss to rock her world.

Barrett pulled her hair from its tidy chignon, running his hands through it, before fisting it firmly, but gently, to tilt her head back. He kissed a path from her lips down her neck, stopping at the pounding pulse in her neck which he licked and sucked gently, just short of leaving a mark.

"Emily, Emily, Emily," he murmured, nuzzling her flushed skin. As his fingers unbuttoned her jacket he bent his head and his hot mouth sought more of her flesh. He reached up to cup her breasts through the silk of her camisole, finding her mouth again, molding the soft flesh in his hands as her nipples beaded greedily into his palms.

She laced her hands around his neck and wedged her knees into the back of the seat to push as close to Barrett as possible, arching her back so that her breasts filled his hands as she rolled her hips over his erection. He groaned against her lips, his teeth grazing her bottom lip as he nipped at her in surprise. She tilted her head back again, and he nuzzled her neck, drunkenly, murmuring her name like a prayer, like he'd never—

"Uh, Kindred Hospital, Mr. Barrett?" Smith's voice over the intercom jolted them both back to reality, and Emily was shocked to realize the town car had stopped. How long had they been parked? And oh, God, did Smith know what they'd been up to in the back, even with the privacy window closed? With their heaving breathing, Emily's moans and whimpers, Barrett's groans, there would be no mistaking what was going on and her cheeks flared with embarrassment as she froze in place, leaning back from Barrett.

Barrett hit a button on console beside him. "Give us two minutes, Smith."

"Roger that."

Barrett's eyes slammed into Emily's, searching and uncertain.

She scrambled off his lap, adjusting her camisole and buttoning her jacket. Her chignon was ruined, but she smoothed her hair with her fingers, before reaching up to touch her lips gingerly. They'd be red and swollen after a make-out session like that, but there was nothing she could do about it now.

"I'm not sorry, Emily." His voice was soft and level, and when she looked up, his eyes were tender.

"Barrett, it was my fault. I shouldn't have asked you—I had no right to ask you to—"

"Do I look like a person easily coerced into doing something he doesn't want to do?"

She ran her fingers through her hair again as Barrett straightened his tie and swiped the back of his hand across his mouth slowly. Even that slight movement made her breath hitch, made her latent panting slightly more pronounced.

She looked down at the glistening ring on her finger, the way the crystal caught the light. It looked so much like a real diamond, for a moment she wondered if it was. She'd gotten so distracted, she'd almost forgotten her mission for tonight, but now she remembered. Emily had been determined to return the ring because she was sure he didn't care for her. And though she wasn't as certain about his indifference to her anymore, after a kiss like that, Emily couldn't possibly accept money from Barrett anymore. Whatever happened next, working for him as his fake fiancée simply wasn't possible.

Emily wiggled the ring over her knuckles and held it out to Barrett, her fingers lightly shaking as it plopped into his hand.

"I'm sorry, I—I can't be your fake fiancée anymore," she whispered. Then she opened her door and hurried out of the car before he could say a word.

Chapter 5

Her perfume lingered in the air around him, as Barrett looked down at the ring in his hand.

What the hell just happened?

He held the ring up to the light from the hospital building. Unbeknownst to Emily, it was a princess cut diamond that had cost him over thirty thousand dollars. He couldn't stomach the idea of Emily wearing some gaudy fake, so he'd purchased the real deal, convincing himself he could always sell the diamond back for fair market value later.

It was still warm from her skin, and he slipped it over his pinkie finger, watching the facets sparkle. Speaking of different facets, Barrett was starting to get whiplash.

He sat back in his seat, waiting until his body calmed down before following her inside, and took an overview approach to the evening so far.

They'd started out the evening with familiar, businesslike formality.

She'd decided to veer from their agreed-upon roles, creating an engagement fantasy for the amusement of Hélène Harrison. (He grudgingly gave her credit for establishing a more stable social rapport with the Harrisons that would certainly grease his deal.)

She got up from the table visibly upset by the course of the engagement fantasy that she herself had concocted and perpetuated.

Upon her return she made hasty farewells, due to upsetting news about the state of her mother's health.

At her request, she ended up on his lap, setting his whole body on fire as she kissed him like the world was ending. (In fairness, he'd given as good as he got.)

She broke up with him. (As much as one can break off an engagement that was fake in the first place.)

The overview approach, which was generally so effective for figuring out where a business deal had gone south, was of no use to him, he thought, running his hands through his hair in frustration. He didn't know why she'd decided to create an engagement fantasy, what about it had upset her, why she wanted him to kiss her so badly when she'd never been interested in him before tonight, and—most baffling of all—why she had just truncated their arrangement without cause.

"Damn it!" he bellowed, disliking the unfamiliarity of being out of his depth and in the dark. Especially with Emily, with whom he'd just shared the most sexually meaningful event of his entire life. And they hadn't even come close to having sex.

His body, which had been cooperating with the plan to "calm down" hardened appreciably at that thought, and Barrett drummed his fingers on the windowsill with annoyance, trying to push the image of naked Emily out of his head.

He was grateful for the distraction when his phone buzzed.

The first message was from Emily:

> Dr. Knightly is here. We cannot thank you enough for your kindness in calling him. My mother is sleeping soundly, but we are concerned about the reason for her blackout. Please don't wait for me. I will go home with my father. —E

Barrett narrowed his eyes, irritated at being dismissed and further annoyed that he was irrelevant to the situation now. Mostly because he wanted to help more. He wanted to be a part of whatever was going on in Emily's life, especially if it pertained to her mother's health.

He grumbled as he pulled up the second message:

> Hélène and I pray that your future mother-in-law recovers quickly from her accident. Emily was a pure delight. We are having a house party at our place in the Hamptons this weekend and Hélène wonders if you two might be free to join us? We'll carve out time to finalize our business. —J.J. Harrison

Great. Fantastic. Just perfect.

In order to solidify the deal Emily's antics had helped to move along, he was going to have to somehow convince her to go to the Hamptons with him next weekend, which would be a feat, since she'd just broken off their fake engagement.

A small part of him was pissed off. They'd just shared the most amazing kiss of his entire life, and she'd chosen that moment to return his ring and run. It didn't just piss him off—if he was honest, he'd admit that it hurt his feelings.

And now, despite her wish to cease and desist playing his fiancée, he needed her more than ever.

He thought of the crappy little apartment that she lived in with her roommate, Valeria Campanile. He knew that they had trouble occasionally meeting their rent because the check had been late more than once, and at least twice it had been drawn from an account owned by Fredo Campanile, Valeria's father. Barrett knew this because when he found out where Emily lived, he'd purchased the building for twice its value from the owner. Emily didn't know that he was actually her landlord. She didn't need to. It gave Barrett peace of mind to know that she'd never be evicted, and he'd had a top of the line security system added to the walk-up as his first order of business.

His father was fond of saying that necessity was the mother of invention. Barrett needed Emily to come with him to the Hamptons for business, yes, but Barrett also wanted time with her. He needed time to explore what had happened between them tonight.

He grimaced as a simple plan laid itself out before him. He didn't like it, but it was certainly a means to an end.

He pressed the button on the console. "Smith, take me to Haverford Park for tonight."

As the car started moving he opened a new text box and started typing his instructions.

Emily woke up the next morning in her childhood bedroom on the second floor of the small gatehouse at Haverford Park. Morning light filtered through the dormer windows that had been decorated with white eyelet curtains for as long as Emily could remember. The red, orange, and brown leafed branches of an oak tree bobbed peacefully just outside her window.

Rolling over, she took her iPhone off the bedside table and checked it for messages. Huh. Two from Valeria and both seemed urgent:

Where are you? Is everything okay?

Pls call & let me know u r ok. Assuming everything went better than expected w/Barrett, u slut. BTW, we need to tlk about $$. New asshole landlord raised rent.

Emily groaned, leaning back and staring at the ceiling. She'd returned the fake engagement ring to Barrett last night, effectively breaking up with him. Damn it, but that had been a hasty decision. She hadn't even considered what would happen if they needed extra money.

She shivered under the covers, stretching languorously then reaching under her shirt to rest her hands flat on her belly. Without thinking, she slid them up to her bare breasts, which she cupped in her palms, her body turning on, instantly hot and wet as she remembered Barrett touching her through the flimsy material of her cami and bra. Her nipples tightened, throbbing for his touch as she slipped another hand into her pajama bottoms, touching herself in the hidden folds behind a trim triangle of fuzz. She remembered the way his tongue felt in her mouth, how his erection had pressed against her belly as he explored her lips and seduced her tongue, touching her, feeling her, branding her. She came to a quick climax with her head full of Barrett, panting softly. Who knew that underneath his cold-blooded, shark exterior, Barrett burned as hot as a bonfire?

Her phone dinged again to alert her to a new message, and she slipped her hands away from her body, an optimistic part of her hoping it was Barrett.

No luck. Valeria again:

Seriously. Need to know u r ok. Combed the lease. Looks like this is lawful, but I'm pissed. I'm going to track down the landlord and give him a piece of my mind!

Emily grinned, typing back:

If anyone can get to the bottom of this, it's you, tiger.

I'm fine. My mother had an accident last night and Barrett drove me out to Haverford. Also, I quit/broke up with him.

How bad is the rent? Do I need to grovel for my job back?

She lay back on the pillow, her thoughts turning to her mother.

Thankfully, Dr. Knightly had been very encouraging the night before, and finally sent Emily and her father home around midnight, insisting that Susannah was stable and they should get some sleep. He said he would call as soon as Susannah's test results came back, but all around, his attitude was reassuring and he told them not to worry, just to come back and visit tomorrow afternoon.

And of course thoughts of Dr. Knightly led directly to thoughts of Barrett again—how he'd called his friend, Victoria, and arranged for the best neurologist in the city to attend to Susannah. It made her heart swell. She sighed, wondering if her feelings for him were welcome. He'd surprised her so much last night, she couldn't discount the possibility that something real had finally flared up between them.

The way he'd played along with the fake engagement story, embellishing it, making her blush, the way he'd said, *"Emily sometimes forgets the romantic hidden deep inside of me."* She bit her lip, feeling weak as she pictured his perfect smile, intense blue eyes and thick blond hair. Was there any truth to that line? *Was* there a romantic hidden deep inside of Barrett and did he have any genuine feelings for her?

The kiss they'd shared had blown her mind, making her hungry—starving, even—for more of him. She'd never experienced chemistry like that with anyone, not in her entire life. Just thinking about it made her feel feverish and exhausted, desperate and longing.

"Barrett," she whispered, flipping over, remembering the way his eyes had softened during their engagement ruse, and her realization that he'd looked at her that way once before.

Her vanity was still covered with photos from her childhood and adolescence, tucked in between the frame and glass of the mirror and her eyes lazily sailed over them, pulled effortlessly to the one on the bottom left, which was mostly obscured by others. Emily got out of bed and sat down at the vanity, plucking the photo carefully away from the glass and staring at it with new eyes: It was a black and white picture of a little boy holding a baby, and Emily knew from countless retellings that it was Barrett holding her a few days after she was born. She could see how the little boy who'd held her so many years ago had grown into the man he was today in his sandy blond hair and the shape of his face, in the strong curve of his jaw, even as a child. She traced the lines of his face with her fingers, almost expecting the photo to animate and for him to look up at her with his bright blue eyes.

She sighed, flipping the picture over to read in her mother's familiar cursive: *Barrett and Emily, when she was new.*

Her shoulders slumped and she wished she understood what was happening between them. As she gazed back at the photo, she wondered again if there could actually be something real growing between her and Barrett, and for the first time, she wondered if maybe it was the sort of thing she'd been looking for, for as long as she could remember.

After two short knocks, the door to Barrett's room swung open and he felt her weight on his bed before he even turned to look at her.

"Good morning."

"I'm asleep," he mumbled.

"Like hell."

"You kiss your father with that mouth?" he asked, a smile pulling at the corners of his.

"I kissed *your* father with that mouth," she retorted. "At least five times."

"Ugh! Mom! Gross!"

He turned over to see his mother, fifty-five-year-old Eleanora Watters English perched on the edge of his bed, dressed sharply in tennis whites. Good genes and excellent self-care had ensured that his mother looked about fifteen years younger than her true age. She worked hard to keep herself in top-notch condition, playing tennis several times a week, walking the extensive grounds of Haverford Park, and volunteering for myriad charities.

"Hello, first-born," she crooned, chucking him under the chin. "To what do I owe this unexpected delight?"

"Long story."

"One that Fitz has already previewed for me, which leads me to enquire: Does that story have anything to do with a certain gardener's daughter?"

Barrett sighed, rubbing his eyes. "And if it does?"

"Take care, eldest," his mother warned, her eyes wary. "These sorts of things can get dicey quick. Felix is very important to your father."

It was interesting to Barrett that his mother always excused herself from a personal relationship with the Edwards, but he understood why. His father, Tom, had grown up with Felix, who had been an early playmate to Barrett's father, an only child. And although Tom English and Felix Edwards rarely socialized formally, it wasn't unusual to see Tom stop by the greenhouse for a quick chat or walk the gardens with Felix in conversation for an hour or more. Barrett's father had even paid for Emily's undergraduate course of study at U Penn as a favor to the Edwards, and though "friends" would be an awkward definition for their relationship, they were certainly very fond of each other.

There was an implicit awkwardness in the situation—her gardener was also her husband's oldest childhood friend and more of a constant in his life than she could rival. The dynamic had created a natural distance between his mother and the Edwards, whom she'd always treated with a mixture of businesslike crispness sprinkled with a bit of familial fondness.

Barrett's mother was young and bouncy when she met ten-years-older Tom English skiing at Vail thirty-three years ago. She had, quite possibly, been on the hunt for a little old money, then surprised herself in discovering that she'd actually fallen in love with Tom. She went from being a very young trophy wife to a very young mother in the first ten months of their marriage, and her five rowdy sons had kept her on her toes.

"Yes, Felix is very important to father. Which is why it was so touching to see you both offering your support at the hospital last night," Barrett answered drily with one raised eyebrow.

"We were at the Graves' house until the wee hours for bridge, brat of mine. We didn't even know Susannah had fallen until we returned home after midnight. Poor thing. I called over to Kindred right away and sent two dozen roses to arrive this morning." She cocked her head to the side, her blue eyes bright and inquisitive. "You know your father would move heaven or earth for Felix, Barrett, which is why you must be careful."

"Hmm."

"Don't 'hmm' at me, Barrett Edward English. You may be thirty-two and a shark of a financier, but I'm still your mother."

"As if I could forget."

"What *are* you doing with Emily Edwards?" she asked directly.

Taking her to dinner. Making up wild fake engagement stories. Kissing her like my life depends on it. His body reacted to his thoughts, and he shifted under the covers.

"Oh, Barrett!" she exclaimed, springing up from his bed. She scrunched up her lips in disapproval and shook her head. "I might have expected this from Alex. But certainly not from you."

"You didn't even let me answer."

She flicked her glance at the sheets disdainfully before returning to his face. "Your, um, *eyes* are telling me all I need to know."

Barrett sighed, sitting up in his bed with his knees to his chest and pulling the comforter up over his bare chest. "It's not what you think."

"Is that so?" She crossed her arms and looked at him squarely. "Emily's a wonderful girl, but use your head, eh, sport? Dabbling with the gardener's daughter isn't exactly a solid plan. Find someone else. Don't let's crap where we eat."

"Alex offered the same eloquent advice."

"Alex is smart. Devious and too charming for his own good, of course. But smart."

Barrett nodded at her, though his mother was wrong. In a million years, Barrett wouldn't dream of "dabbling" with Emily. Like his father's bond with Felix, Barrett's bond with Emily had been forged so many years ago, he didn't remember a time he didn't have true, genuine feelings for her. What he felt had no room for "dabbling." It sailed way beyond "like," floating perilously close to something deeper altogether. Still, one thing Barrett loved about his mother was that she never minced words. She was frothy and cheerful to all outward appearances, but when it came to her sons, she'd always insisted on complete honesty and openness and he respected that.

"I promise no dabbling," he answered with pursed lips, unwilling to fill her in on his feelings until he'd had a chance to figure them out himself.

"And get some sunshine today! You're pale! You work way too hard." She headed for the door. "Weston's around this weekend too, you know. But he's supposed to be studying for the bar so don't bother him." She winked at him and was gone.

He huffed once, feeling his brows crease as he reviewed his mother's warning to stay away from Emily.

Like that's even a choice anymore.

By now her roommate would have gotten the rent notice, and surely Emily would be reconsidering their arrangement. He felt like a cad, but if he was honest with himself—which he had decided was for the best—his reasons for trapping her into being his date next weekend were not solely business-related, but twofold.

One, yes, he legitimately needed her help to cinch the deal. The Harrisons liked her and he needed to close the deal with them. If he showed up without her, it would raise questions about the legitimacy of their engagement, casting shadows on Barrett's honesty and ethics, which he couldn't afford to have happen. He needed Emily to continue playing the part of the imminent Mrs. Barrett English, because it would ensure this deal happened.

Two, he liked her. He *really* liked her. He liked her so much it was squeezing his chest like a vise, and he still wasn't backing away. She was smart and charming and fantastically beautiful, and he had a funny feeling she held his past and his future in the palm of her hand. He wanted a million repeats of last night—he wanted to wake up naked beside her, their limbs loose and tangled as he pulled her against him, and she welcomed him inside. Barrett couldn't remember much of his life before Emily was a beacon on his radar. The reality was that he was accustomed to getting exactly what he wanted, and for as long as Emily Edwards had drawn breath, Barrett English had wanted her.

And for that to happen, the one immediate thing he needed from Emily Edwards was time.

Chapter 6

Emily's mother was awake when they arrived at noon for the start of visiting hours. As her test results came back throughout the afternoon, it turned out that she didn't need a neurologist, after all, but a cardiologist. Susannah had developed stable angina, which had caused her to faint. But with rest and proper medication, she should be able to keep it under control, and the doctors had reassured her that her life could go back to normal. She still had a fairly nasty contusion on her forehead from face-planting on the Englishes' stairs, so the doctors had suggested one more night in the hospital.

By the time Emily and her father returned to Haverford, it was almost five o'clock. Even though her father had offered to take her for a BLT at the Haverford Diner, she wanted him to have a home-cooked meal tonight after the anxiety of the last two days, so they stopped at the grocery store on the way home. Emily picked up ground meat and breadcrumbs for meatballs, tomato sauce, spaghetti and everything she needed for a garden salad. Her father popped a loaf of garlic bread in the cart, and Emily grinned at him, relieved when he grinned back.

"I haven't even asked you about your studies, Emmy," said her father as they drove home.

"They're going really well."

"Awfully expensive, PhD at U Penn."

"Don't worry," she said, knowing he felt bad that he wasn't able to help more. But Emily felt lucky. Mr. and Mrs. English had kindly covered the cost of her undergraduate work, so the cost of her PhD would be a fraction of what she would have owed. And yes, she might be eighty before she paid off her student loans, but damn it, there'd be a PhD beside her name when she did. "I'm student teaching and tutoring, plus I pick up, um, odd jobs here and there. Anyway, it's worth it, Dad."

"Never thought I'd have such a brilliant daughter. You're the first Edwards to go to grad school, Emily Faith, and you'll certainly be the first who has the right to call herself a doctor."

"Hey Dad," she said, cocking her head to the side as she asked the familiar question. "Why'd you decide to become a gardener?"

"That old story?" He sighed, but started telling it again because he knew she loved it as much as any bedtime story. "Well, as you know, I grew up here at Haverford Park, just like you. Watched my granddad and my father both tend the grounds, and I guess I knew every inch of this place like the back of my hand by the time I graduated Penn State at twenty-one with a degree in Horticulture Science. But like most twenty-one-year-old fools, I decided to turn my back on Haverford Park and make my own way.

"I graduated college, thanked Mr. and Mrs. English very much for the free ride, packed everything I owned in a duffel bag, took the money I'd saved from gardening every summer and flew to London. I spent three months backpacking around Europe—"

"Until you met Mama in a garden in Giverny."

"She was sitting there in a peasant blouse with a long skirt and her wavy blonde hair in a bun held back with an extra paintbrush. I sat down on a bench beside her and without even looking at me, she said she wished she knew someone who could cut back the forsythia that was ruining the view she was trying to paint."

"So you went to the store and came back an hour later with a pair of shears."

He grinned. "Scissors. Barber scissors, Emmy. They were all I could find. I cut that yellow bush into a thing of beauty with barber scissors, and when I returned to Philly that Winter, she was my bride."

"And you came home to Haverford Park."

"Yes, I did. My old Dad was aging by that time, so I started taking over little by little until it all belonged to me."

"Who will take over after you?" asked Emily, feeling the familiar guilt that she hadn't been born male to take over for her father as the fourth generation gardener for the English family.

"Don't worry about that. I'll find someone who loves the gardens here just as much as I do. New blood for this little gatehouse." Felix shrugged beside her. "Anyway. That's how I became the gardener."

"I love that story," said Emily quietly, wondering what her own love story would look like from a view of forty years. Would it begin with a man she'd known all of her life, stern and cold, asking her to playact as his fiancée?

"Barrett drove you home last night," her father said, as though reading her thoughts.

"Mm-hm."

"You dating him?"

"It's not really like that."

"You care for him?"

"Oh, Dad." She looked over at her father, wishing she had answers for him. Wishing she had answers for *her*.

"He sent over that fancy doctor last night."

"It's complicated."

"Well, there's no time like the present to uncomplicate things, Emmy . . . especially since he's here waiting for you."

Emily's eyes snapped from her father's profile forward to look through the windshield. A smile took over the entire real estate of her face as she drank in the sight of beautiful, blond, blue-eyed Barrett English, sitting on the bench under a Technicolor oak tree, waiting for her.

"Evening, Barrett."

"Hey, Felix," said Barrett as he stood, holding out his hand and offering a cautious smile. "How's Susannah?"

"She's got angina. She's going to be fine. Thanks for the doc."

"Oh, sure. It was nothing."

"You were always a good kid, Barrett. Stay for dinner. Emily's making spaghetti and meatballs."

"Oh, thanks, I'll uh . . ."

Felix took the sack of groceries out of Emily's arms without a word, then continued into the cottage, letting the door close behind him.

"I didn't know you stayed over last night," said Emily, her cheeks pink. Her eyes darted down his body, taking in his U Penn T-shirt and worn jeans. The slight tilt of her lips told him that she liked what she saw.

Turnabout was fair play, wasn't it? Barrett dragged his eyes slowly and deliberately down her body too. She wore a white button-down tucked into soft-looking jeans, and little black shoes on her feet. On the way back up, he stared at the V in her shirt for an extra minute, then lingered at her lips before finding her eyes again.

She took a deep breath and he could hear the raggedness of it as her chest swelled appealingly.

"Barrett," she said softly in warning, then seemed lost and bit her lower lip as she stared up at him.

"Don't do that," he said in a low voice, "or I'll kiss you again."

"My Dad's right inside. He's probably watching us."

"I don't care who's watching."

Emily released her lip slowly and took another deep breath.

"Your mother's okay?"

Emily nodded.

"You want me to stay for dinner?"

Emily nodded.

"You going to come stargazing with me on the tennis courts later?"

Her eyes widened and she grinned at him, nodding again.

His lips twitched as his heart thumped with the thought of having her all to himself for a little while.

She started toward the little house, but he called out softly to her. "Emily."

She turned back to him, her blue eyes bright and just a little darker than they'd been a moment before. He took two steps toward her until he was so close he could smell Shalimar and feel the heat of her skin.

She was still as he leaned down slowly, deliberately, stopping just short of her ear, his lips grazing the hot skin as he whispered in a low promise, "Whether you bite your lip or not and no matter who's watching, I'm kissing you later."

Emily drew back, searching his eyes as her cheeks flushed. Flicking a glance to his lips before finding his eyes again, she said, "Maybe."

She gave him the sexiest grin he'd ever seen, then turned and followed her father into the house, leaving the door ajar for him.

"Damn," muttered Barrett under his breath, not blinking until she was totally out of sight. How the hell was he supposed to sit through dinner with Felix?

Emily needed her job back.

According to Valeria, with whom she'd been texting as she visited with her mother that afternoon, the rent had been raised by four hundred dollars a month, an almost absurd amount for the modest walk-up they rented in downtown Philly. Neither of them had that sort of money lying around and while Emily's parents were comfortable, they weren't the sort of comfortable that could subsidize Emily's life. And though Valeria's father, who owned a chain of Italian restaurants in Philadelphia, had been kind enough to float them a time or two, this wasn't about being floated for a few days while they scraped together the balance. This was about the girls needing subsequent income to make the rent at all. And while Val said she could go back to moonlighting as a ballroom dancing instructor at her aunt's studio, that wouldn't even net one hundred dollars a week. They both agreed the best way to get it fast was for Emily to continue to "work" for Barrett.

Unfortunately, Emily's recent make-out session with Barrett in the back of the limo made this ethically dicey. It was one thing for Barrett to pay her for her time while she playacted at being his fiancée. But, if she was getting physical with him *and* taking his money? It came perilously close to a different sort of "arrangement" altogether, and Emily just wasn't that kind of girl.

After a long discussion with Valeria, they agreed on two things: one, they needed to move within the next two months to a cheaper place. Valeria would start looking for an apartment whose rent met their combined income from student teaching. And two, Emily would continue to "work" for Barrett just until she'd made the eight hundred dollars they needed to cover the rent for October and November. Both girls agreed she couldn't accept money for last night, and she couldn't fool around with him as long as money exchanged hands, which frustrated Emily. It was going to be almost impossible not to touch Barrett— or *long* to be touched by him—after what they'd shared in the car last night.

Still, if he'd hire her back and give her two easy jobs over the next week or so, she could make her eight hundred dollars and then she'd break up with him for good . . . at which point she'd be one-hundred percent free to start dating him . . . if that's what he wanted. Because Emily knew without a shadow of a doubt if Barrett English actually wanted to be with her, there was nothing in the world that could keep her from him.

Her father headed upstairs to take a shower and clean up before dinner, which left Emily and Barrett in the kitchen alone. Emily mashed the ground beef between her fingers, then wiped them on her mother's apron as she poured in some bread crumbs and cracked an egg into the mixture. Barrett had surprised her by volunteering to help and was dicing onions and garlic on the countertop beside her. What surprised her even more was that he appeared to know what he was doing.

"I didn't know you cooked," she said, throwing an egg shell in the trash and plunging her hands back into the sticky mixture.

Barrett shrugged. "No one really does. But I like to eat good food and takeout gets old. Plus, I think I put together some of my best deals while I'm distracted by making dinner."

Emily looked up at him and grinned. "So, do you only cook for yourself, or . . ."

"Are you asking if I have a girlfriend?"

She felt the heat in her cheeks and looked at the bowl in front of her on the counter. His hip bumped into hers playfully.

"That would be pretty cheeky, seeing as how I had a fake fiancée up until a few hours ago."

"Maybe you cheated on your fake fiancée with your fake girlfriend," she teased. *Or with Felicity Atwell, whatever she is to you.*

He stopped dicing for a moment, turning to face her. "Are you really asking?"

Emily looked up at him quickly and felt herself nodding before she gave herself permission. Barrett stared at her, flicking his glance to her lips, then back to her eyes. She saw his darken, narrow, as the moment took a heavy, serious turn.

"No, Emily," he finally murmured. "I don't have a girlfriend."

Again, without permission, her body reacted. Her lips trembled for a moment before tilting up into a smile. "Oh. Good."

Barrett dropped the knife on the cutting board, letting it clatter into the pile of neatly chopped onions, and reached for her waist, pulling her up against his body. His chest heaved into hers, making her nipples pucker with want. She arched her back a little, pressing into him more intimately.

You haven't been hired back yet! thought Emily a little desperately. *Kiss him now while you still can!*

If she thought about it, she'd talk herself out of it, so instead she leaned up quickly on her tiptoes and pressed her lips to his. She could tell she had surprised him, because for a moment, he was frozen. But then she wound her hands around his neck, flipping them so that the clean backs pressed up against his skin. She brushed her tongue softly along the seam of his lips. That's all it took. That's all.

Barrett growled into her mouth, grasping her hips and lifting her like a doll onto the kitchen counter. The bowl skidded backwards against the wall as he stepped between her legs. She wrapped them around his back, crossing her ankles together around his waist as his tongue swept into her mouth. His fingers fisted against the denim of her backside, and she pushed aggressively into his chest as he sucked on her tongue. Leaning her head to the side, he skimmed his way down her neck with his lips, sucking and licking as she moaned softly, her eyes closed and her head resting on the cabinets behind her.

"Barrett," she whispered, and he returned his lips to hers, nibbling lightly on the top, then the bottom, before exploring her mouth with his tongue again. And Emily realized she was a fool if she thought she could pose as Barrett's fiancée and not touch him. It would be impossible. They couldn't even keep their hands to themselves while making meatballs, for heaven's sake. But she needed the money. She needed it. She couldn't be evicted.

Using every bit of strength, she pulled her mouth away from his, leaning back against the cabinets. "My father . . ." she murmured. "The water just went off."

Barrett panted in front of her, his eyes dazed and confused, like she was speaking an alien language. His chest swelled with every breath, but Emily caved backwards, so her breasts no longer touched him. If they did, she'd reach for him again. She slid her ankles down and dropped her hands from the back of his neck.

"Jesus, Emily. Just . . . give me a minute." He leaned his head forward, bracing his hands on the counter on either side of her hips. "I wasn't expecting that."

"Sorry," she mumbled.

His head snapped up, and his eyes were focused and hungry. "Don't *ever* say you're sorry for touching me. Never."

She opened her mouth to say something, but every thought flew from her head from the way Barrett was looking at her. She bit her lip instead, and his eyes zeroed in on that small move like a tractor beam.

"Emily," he growled in warning.

With a small popping sound she let go of her lip, but it was too late. He leaned forward, catching it between his teeth gently, tugging on it. It was the only place their bodies touched, but it sent a shock of heat from her mouth straight down to her belly until it pooled in her stomach making her insides clench and tighten with longing for him. Her eyes closed and she whimpered lightly as his lips landed flush on hers, his hands tilting up from the counter to hold her hips tightly.

Barrett must have heard the sound of footsteps on the stairs before she did, because he pulled back abruptly, muttering "Damn it" and picking up the knife without a word. Still panting softly, he kept his head down as he resumed his place in front of the cutting board. Emily was still perched on the counter a second later when her father entered the kitchen.

"You want a beer, Barrett? Emily, get off the counter. Your mother would have a fit."

Emily looked quickly at Barrett as she hopped down, noticing that he was smiling down at the cutting board as her father scolded her.

"I'd love one, Felix. Thanks."

"What about me, Dad? Beer for men only?"

"Emily Faith," he said, turning from the frig with three beers hooked through his fingers, "I didn't ask, because I already knew what your answer would be."

"Women were the prime brewers of beer in medieval Europe, you know."

"I know," answered her father patiently, pulling three frosty glasses from a collection at the back of the small freezer.

"Even by the seventeen hundreds, over seventy-eight percent of the brewers in England were still women."

"Yup," said her father, popping the caps off the bottles.

"And in colonial times, here in America, women still appeared as tavern-keepers, many of whom brewed their own beer."

Emily looked to her left and Barrett was standing with his back to the counter, grinning at her. "Why do you know so much about beer?"

Felix handed cold glasses to Emily and Barrett, then fixed his eyes on Barrett. "How much do you know about Emmy's PhD?"

Barrett looked a little chagrined, glancing at her then back at her father. "Not a lot."

"Ask her to tell you about it sometime." Her father raised his glass, winking at Emily. "To Emmy, who knows more about beer than any woman I ever met."

Emily cocked her head to the side and grinned at Barrett as they clinked their glasses together and drank.

Over dinner Barrett learned that part of Emily's planned dissertation would focus on how England's shift from ale to beer brewing illustrated the transition from a traditional agricultural economy to a capitalist market economy, and how women were slowly edged out of the process. She intended to use this historical shift to show how women were the basis for most businesses in society and only sidelined by men when the established business became successful.

Now, Barrett respected the entirety of her thesis—he had a healthy respect for women in the finance industry and treated women with the same cutthroat tactics he did men—but he was a little ashamed that the thought that kept running through his head was this: *My super smart girl studies beer.* If there was anything—*anything*—sexier than that, Barrett couldn't possibly imagine what it was . . . until Emily started describing the process of home-brewing beer. She talked about boiling short batches of hops and other grains, combining the water in a large barrel and cooling it down in a chiller, which pretty much would've been her nickname if they'd gone to college together.

Apparently Emily and her father brewed a new batch of Edwards Select every summer, and the beer they were presently drinking was one of their own IPAs. He watched Emily and Felix bounce off each other so effortlessly, and fleetingly wished he'd spent more time visiting with them in the little gatehouse while he was growing up.

"Well, Emmy, excellent dinner, as always."

"My *sous chef* helped," she said, gesturing open-palmed to Barrett, who lifted his glass and toasted her before sipping. Dinner had been a great distraction, and thoroughly enjoyable, but he was anxious to get her alone.

As though Felix could read his thoughts, he leaned forward, and piled the three plates together. "Why don't you two go for a walk or something? Still warm enough, huh?"

Barrett looked at Emily across the candlelit table. She reached over and touched the back of her father's hand. "It's okay, Dad. We'll stay and help clean up."

"No, Miss. You made the dinner. You don't have to go for a walk if you're not up for it, but either way, I'll take care of the dishes. Solo. It's only fair."

"Come on, Emily," said Barrett, winking at her. "We'll get some fresh air."

"I'll grab a sweater," she said, hopping up from her place and setting a little kiss on a bald spot on the top of her father's head before sprinting to the stairs.

"She's quite a girl," said Felix, looking up at Barrett.

"No argument here," said Barrett carefully, feeling the shift from Felix, his family's gardener, to Felix, Emily's protective father. Barrett adjusted accordingly from son of the manor to prospective suitor, anxious to assure Felix that his intentions toward Emily were totally and completely aboveboard.

"I don't know what you two are up to, Barrett . . . and I have to say, if it was Alex who'd driven her home last night I sure wouldn't have invited him for dinner, no matter how many doctors he called."

Barrett inclined his head once, holding Felix's steady gaze. "I appreciate that, sir."

"You've never given me reason to question your judgment. You were always a serious kid. Hard worker. Tough businessman. Your Dad's plenty proud of you."

Barrett forced himself not to look away, though accepting compliments was always difficult for him.

"But if you're not serious about her, I'd just as soon you walk away. Right now. When she comes back down the stairs, I'll just tell her you got a phone call and had to head back to the main house. I'm not asking if you plan to marry her, son, but she's not one to trifle with either."

"Understood, Felix." Barrett nodded, sitting back in his chair deliberately. "I'm not going anywhere."

"All right then," said Felix, his face neither happy nor unhappy as he reached across the table to take the unused silverware and pile it on top of the dirty plates. But his blue eyes were shrewd as they caught Barrett's before turning into the kitchen. "As long as we're clear, Barrett."

"We're clear, sir."

Emily's footsteps on the creaky stairs made Barrett stand up, and then there she was, standing in the doorway of the tiny dining room, a soft pink sweater covering her white shirt, and her blonde hair down from its ponytail. Her lips were shiny, and she was wearing a gold necklace. He got a whiff of Shalimar as she put her hands on her hips and grinned at him. If there was a prettier, sweeter, smarter girl on the face of the earth, Barrett English had yet to meet her.

"Ready to go stargazing?" he asked, offering her his hand.

"Ready as I'll ever be," she answered, letting him pull her out the side door, into the cool of the evening.

Chapter 7

Haverford Park was a grand estate, equal to any other on the Philadelphia Main Line, in Newport, Rhode Island, or in the Hudson Valley of New York.

Even having grown up there, Emily still managed to be surprised by its awesome beauty every time she returned home. Her father tended the grounds carefully with his staff of four, and there were dozens of gardens throughout the property, in addition to fountains, porches and patios, stone benches in charming copses, an outdoor pool, tennis courts, a putting green, and a game lawn for croquet or cricket, a game which the English family hosted annually as part of their Summer Party. Every English son was an excellent cricket player.

Emily and Barrett walked up the well-lit white gravel driveway toward the main house, hand-in-hand, before Barrett pulled her through one of the arched openings in the high hedges. Emily knew the way to the tennis courts with her eyes closed, but there was something magical about letting Barrett lead the way, inviting her from the gatehouse to the grounds of the main house. There was something about it that she liked very much.

And she wondered, again, how to get her job back without losing whatever was going on between them, because what she really wanted to do was to press pause and come right back to this minute in a week or two, as soon as she'd made eight hundred dollars. Come right back here. Back here to perfect.

They walked slowly across the game lawn in the twilight saying nothing. It smelled of fall—the dueling smells of fresh cut grass and the burning wood in a nearby fireplace—and Emily thought that if she had to remember one perfect moment for the rest of her life, it would be this one. Her mother's health wasn't in danger. Her father had been funny and loving over dinner, occasionally shooting a brief, concerned glance between her and Barrett, but otherwise leaving her to make her own choices and live her own life. And Barrett English, with whom she'd been deeply infatuated for most of her life, was holding her hand, walking beside her in the dying light, like maybe there was space in his life for her. It didn't matter that her rent had been raised or that she was getting behind on her studies as she spent the weekend in Haverford. It didn't matter that he was an English and she was an Edwards. Nothing mattered except right here and right now with Barrett, and Emily wanted to soak up every second.

When they got to the tennis courts, Barrett dropped her hand and took two lounge chair cushions off two chaises and dragged them to the center of the courts. He gestured to them and Emily lay down on one while he lay down beside her, and they were still, side-by-side, as the inky sky grew darker.

"Can I ask you something?" Barrett finally asked, breaking the silence.

"Sure."

"Do you even *like* Riesling?"

Emily chuckled. "No."

"You'd prefer a beer, wouldn't you?"

"Always."

"Then why didn't you ever say anything?"

"Why in the world did you think I liked Riesling?"

"Because that's what you drank . . . that night on the trampoline."

"You weren't hanging out with us. I'm surprised you remember a detail like that."

He shrugged. "I wasn't sitting on the trampoline with you, but I was there. I was home for the weekend."

"I remember. You came out to yell at us."

"That's what you remember?"

"Was there more?"

"I walked you and Daisy back to the gatehouse at two o'clock in the morning."

"I don't remember that."

"I'm not surprised."

"We were drunk as skunks. I imagine you were very disapproving."

"I was."

"Better I don't remember then."

"Stuffy Barrett, right?"

She heard a very slight edge slip into his voice. "I didn't say that."

"I was jealous," he whispered, his fingers moving lightly beside hers, tentatively reaching out, then lacing their hands together firmly when she didn't pull away.

"You were? Why? Of what? You were all grown up, in grad school and—"

"And you were this gorgeous fifteen-year-old hanging out with three of my younger brothers, and I hated their guts for it. I hated myself too. You were just a kid. I had no business thinking about you like that."

"Like what?" she whispered, staring up at the night sky, every cell of her body aware of the slow circles his thumb was making against her hand.

He raised her hand to his lips and brushed them against her skin softly, before lowering their joined hands to his chest. She could feel the fierce pounding of his heart beneath her fingers, and it matched the galloping of hers.

She swallowed, pushing thoughts of dating Barrett legitimately out of her mind, no matter how much she wanted to think about it. She needed money. She needed to get her job back before things between them went any further.

"Barrett," she started, rolling her neck to look at him on the pillow beside her. "I shouldn't have given you back the ring last night and quit. That was . . . hasty."

His heart plummeted. He'd been about to tell her . . .

Like the only girl who existed on the face of the earth. Like the only girl who ever mattered. Like the only girl I ever wanted.

He swallowed his disappointment, reminding himself of Harrison Shipbuilding, and that by raising her rent, he'd actually been the one to engineer her need for further employment. If anyone was confusing things between them, it was him. It still stung, though, because it made him wonder if everything they'd shared tonight had been premeditated on her part to get her job back.

Well, it didn't matter. He needed her this weekend, regardless of how she felt. And after he solidified things with J.J. Harrison, he'd lower the rent and tell her he didn't want her to work for him anymore. He'd tell her that a part of him had always been in love with her and he wanted her to be his real girlfriend. And God willing what they'd been flirting with since last night wasn't just an act and she wanted to be with him as much as he wanted to be with her. As for losing her income source, well, once they were a couple, if she ever needed his help—financially or otherwise—all she'd need to do is ask.

"You want me to hire you back?"

"Do you have any upcoming jobs?"

"In fact, I do," he said, releasing her hand and lacing his own together to pillow them under his head. He didn't trust himself not to reach for her, but he only wanted her to accept his touch if she really liked him. And right now? He couldn't tell if she liked him or needed his money.

"So . . . ?" she prompted.

"The Harrisons, actually. They're having a house party out in the Hamptons next weekend. Friday afternoon to Sunday afternoon. There will be polo and parties, boat trips and business. They specifically asked about you and hoped we could come together if your mother had recuperated by then."

"A whole weekend?" she asked softly.

"Two nights."

"And what would you . . . pay me?"

He heard the wince in her voice, and he hated it, and he hated himself for putting it there, but forced himself to respond. This was business, after all, and he needed her. "For a whole weekend? One thousand dollars. If the deal closes before we leave, five hundred more. As a bonus."

Her breath, which she must have been holding, came out in a rush. "Whew! That's a lot of money."

Not for me, he thought. *I'd pay ten times as much to have you by my side for a weekend.*

That's something else Barrett hadn't been totally honest about.

The whole reason Barrett had approached Emily in the first place wasn't because he had a board meeting at U Penn and had run into her by happenstance, but because he'd overheard his father and Felix talking one afternoon as they walked the gardens together. His father had asked about Emily and Felix had confided that he was concerned about her mounting expenses. Felix had overheard her on the phone with Valeria, arranging for Valeria's father to help them with their rent one month. Felix and Susannah were not the sort of parents to swoop in and give Emily a free ride, but Barrett couldn't stand the idea that she was struggling. He couldn't help but figure out his own way to offer her a little extra income. So, he'd found out where she'd be and he'd "stumbled" across her one May afternoon.

"Is that a yes?"

"Yes, I'll take the job," said Emily in a small voice. "I'll ask Valeria to teach my class on Friday afternoon."

"I'll arrange for a small plane to take us out and back. It'll be a quick trip."

"Fine," she answered, shifting subtly away from him on her cushion . . . and he hated it.

"And I owe you four hundred dollars for last night."

"No."

He turned his head to look at her. "What? Why not? You earned every—"

"No, Barrett. I can't accept anything for last night."

Of course. He understood. She didn't feel that she deserved it for taking that risk with the engagement charade. He hurried to correct her. "I have to admit, I didn't like the whole engagement story silliness at first, but I have to say, it worked in my benefit, Emily. The Harrisons were—"

"Not because of that."

He narrowed his eyes at her stony profile, lifting up on his elbow to get a better look at her face. "I don't understand."

She cleared her throat. "We, um, we *made out* last night. In the car."

"Yes." *And it was the best kiss. Anywhere. Ever.* "I remember."

"So I can't accept any money from you, Barrett!" she snapped.

"Because we *made out.*"

"Yes."

"You won't accept money from me because we made out," he repeated.

Ohhhhhh.

He said the words again in his head, and they finally made sense to him, and just as they did, a terrible realization occurred to him. Barrett's mind, which was sharp as a tack in business negotiations, realized the unintended consequence—indeed, the unintended, personally *catastrophic* consequence—to their proposed arrangement just one second too late.

He'd fixed things so she needed money. But if she came to the Hamptons as his employee, she wouldn't let him touch her. So essentially he had just arranged to spend a weekend in the Hamptons with the girl of his dreams, sharing a bedroom, playacting at fiancé, no doubt turned-on to the point of pain, without the slightest chance of being able to sleep with her. *Damn, damn, damn.*

"Are you saying that if you come to the Hamptons with me as my fake fiancée, this—whatever is going on between us—is over?"

"Just on hold," she confirmed in a small voice.

And that's when Barrett "the Shark" English realized that all of his business acumen and training were no match against Emily Edwards, because he strenuously considered texting J.J. Harrison to go screw himself, turning his back on the deal and carrying Emily to his bedroom.

"And then?" he asked, staring down at her, searching her eyes with what must have been wild longing. "When we get home from the Harrisons'?"

She shrugged lightly. "We'll see."

"We'll see *what* exactly?" he asked tightly, his hard body frustrated to the point of desperation at the idea of not touching Emily from now until next Monday.

"What happens next. What we want."

"I already know what I want," he said softly, leaning down to brush his lips against hers. "It's the same thing I've wanted forever."

"Then waiting an extra week shouldn't matter," she said, turning her head away.

"I haven't given you the ring back. Technically you're not working for me again yet. What about tonight?"

He brushed the soft strands of light hair away from her ear. When he leaned down and took her earlobe between his teeth gently, he heard her breath hitch.

"I already agreed to the job."

"Emily," he whispered against her hot skin. "One kiss."

She turned back to look up at him and her eyes were glistening with tears. "I don't want to muddy the waters, Barrett. I don't want to confuse things. I . . ." Her breath was ragged against his lips as she exhaled shakily, nodding. "One kiss."

Then she reached up and placed her palm against his cheek, pulling his head down to hers.

Emily knew that she had no business making out with him. She'd agreed to do one last job for him and until that job was over, it would confuse things for them to be intimate with one another. But he'd never been so forthcoming about his feelings before, and it made her frustrated and desperate to think that after tonight she wouldn't be able to touch him again for at least a week . . . if not forever. The reality was that they'd made no promises to one another—nothing beyond this night was guaranteed, and if tonight was all she had with Barrett English, she wanted it to count.

Barrett rolled on top of her, cradling her face in his hands as his weight settled, pushing her body into the plush cushion below. One of his legs wedged between hers, while the other fell slightly onto the pliant turf of the court beneath them. His pelvis lined up with hers and she could feel the hard bulge of his erection through his jeans, pushing insistently against her softness. She shifted slightly, arching her back a little to better cradle him there. His solid chest crushed her breasts beneath him, and his elbows made indents in the cushion above her shoulders.

He leaned his head down, his nose in the curve of her neck as his hair flopped over his forehead, pressing his lips to her throbbing pulse, sucking and kissing as his hot breath fanned out across her neck. Shivers raised hairs on Emily's arms as she closed her eyes, memorizing the feel of his lips against her skin and wishing this moment with him never needed to end. She wished they could forget about rent and deals, about fake engagements . . . and just be together, start something real with each other tonight.

Barrett shifted, brushing his lips from her throat to her ear, bracing on his elbows and sliding up her body. Her nipples beaded from the light friction, and she hooked one leg over his ass as he thrust forward against her, simulating sex. Emily arched her back again, grabbing the back of his neck and pulling his lips to hers roughly and moaning into his mouth as he threaded his hands through her hair and kissed her.

And *kissed* her.

Oh, my God, how he kissed her.

His teeth grazed hers as he sought out her tongue and sucked it into his mouth, fiercely claiming her, branding her, maybe even punishing her a little because they both knew it would feel like years until they could kiss each other again. He rolled his body to her side, propping himself up with one elbow, but letting his other hand rest, flat and heavy in the V of exposed skin at the base of her throat. He kept kissing her as that hand slid lower, working the buttons of her shirt nimbly, unfastening them as Emily's tongue explored his mouth, leisurely dipping into its crevasses, finding the hidden parts of Barrett. So much of Barrett was new to her, and yet so much was still familiar, Emily was overwhelmed by the dueling sensations of comfort and risk, which made her feel scared and safe, set adrift while firmly anchored. It made her breathless. It made her brave.

She bowed her back and Barrett reached under her to unclasp her bra, then opened her shirt, the cool air touching her hot skin like a blessing. He skimmed his mouth over her chin, tracing the lines of her throat with his lips. His hands reached for her breasts, molding them gently through the loosened fabric of her bra and she whimpered, wanting more of him, wanting the skin of his hands on the skin of her breasts, with nothing else between them. She leaned her head back into the cushion, biting her lower lip, her fingers twisting into the coarse fabric by her sides in anticipation as he pushed her bra up and over her breasts, baring them to the night.

"Emily," he whispered, his breath hot on her chest, the stubble from his beard rasping against her skin as he dipped his head lower.

She heard the reverence in his voice, and the question. She knew what he was asking, and she knew that they'd need to stop soon. But not yet. God, please not yet. She moved her hands to the back of his head, gently pushing his head lower until she felt the heat of his mouth hover over one throbbing nipple.

And then his lips came down, hot and teasing, over her puckered flesh as he sucked the hardened bead into the hot, wet heaven of his mouth. The sensation was so sharp, such torture and such relief that she bucked up against him. His hand steadied her, closing around the flesh of her breast to hold her in his mouth while he licked and kissed, sucking firmly, then blowing softly as Emily flinched and moaned, her head thrashing lightly as he moved to her other breast. His hand stayed on the breast he'd just loved, softly rolling the erect nipple within his thumb and forefinger, as he took its twin into his mouth. The wet heat combined with the tug of his lips on the tightened bud, and darts of pleasure shot straight to the muscles hidden deep between her thighs which flexed and contracted, every nerve ending firing from the intense sensation of Barrett loving her body.

She could barely catch her breath, and her heart beat the primitive rhythm shared by every woman to whom the man of her dreams makes love . . .

More, more, more.

His hand slid down her stomach, under the waistband of her jeans, resting tentatively over the white cotton of her panties as his mouth continued torturing her with pleasure, flicking his tongue over the hard tip of her nipple, making her flinch and shudder beneath him. She knew it was time to turn back, to tell Barrett they needed to stop here and save the rest for the night they returned from the Hamptons, but two fingers slipped into the waistband of her panties, and she lost the ability to make a coherent decision.

He shifted back to her other nipple, groaning against her skin, "You're so wet for me, Emily. So hot and wet." Emily bit her lip, arching up against his fingers as they parted her hidden flesh and found their mark—the throbbing nub of firm flesh that wanted, that demanded, his touch.

She gasped as one of his long fingers stroked her, the rhythm somehow matching the way his tongue caressed her breasts. The hot, insistent pooling in her stomach spread like wildfire through her veins, flushing her body, which glowed with sweat and teemed with goose bumps, as Barrett abandoned her breasts for her lips. Her fingers curled aggressively into his hair, pulling and scraping as he cupped her face with his free palm and whispered against her lips, "I want you to come for me, Emily. Now."

He'd invited her to go stargazing.

Emily saw stars.

The command, delivered in Barrett's taut, low voice, was all it took for her to let go completely, her muscles convulsing as she bucked up against his hand, and he swallowed her cries. He gently stroked the turgid flesh under his fingers until the pulsing slowed and her shudders softly subsided. Then he pulled her shirt loosely over her breasts to shield her skin from the cool night air and lay his head on her chest, listening to the wild pounding of her heart.

Chapter 8

"Fix it, Stratton. I can't do everything, damn it!"

"Jesus, you've been a prick this week," exclaimed Barrett's younger brother. "And just as a reminder? You may be the Chief Operating Officer, Barrett, but Dad's still the President even if he *is* in Zurich for two weeks. You're not the top asshole yet."

"I may as well be," Barrett grumbled. "I do everything around here."

Stratton stood from the chair in front of Barrett's desk and straightened his glasses. Stratton was, and had always been, the most bookish and serious of the brothers. He was in charge of researching future acquisitions, and his projected numbers looked accurate. Barrett just didn't like them.

"May as well be *top asshole*? Yeah. You're definitely acting like it, anyway."

Stratton slammed Barrett's office door behind him, leaving Barrett and Fitz alone.

Fitz, who'd been listening from the couch where he was reviewing the final Harrison Shipbuilding documents before drawing up tentative contracts for the acquisition, didn't look up. "He's right, you know. You're being an asshole. I mean, more than usual."

"Screw you, Fitz," said Barrett, swiveling in his chair to look out at the Philadelphia skyline.

He wondered where Emily was, who she was with, if she was smiling or studying or taking a nap. He couldn't stop thinking about her and while it hadn't affected his work yet, it was definitely messing with his familial relationships.

"Yeah. Screw me. Okay. But, I'm the last brother standing." Fitz cleared his throat, and though Barrett didn't turn back around, he knew his brother had moved to one of the chairs in front of Barrett's desk because his voice was closer when he spoke again. "Alex won't come back in here after your tantrum on Tuesday morning. Weston, who was working *for free*, refuses to do anymore paralegal moonlighting until you take back what you said about him being the 'idiot savant' of the family, and I think you just managed the impossible: you pissed off Stratton."

Barrett took a deep breath and sighed, turning around. Fitz and Stratton, sandwiched between the first, middle, and last English brothers, had always been a little quieter than the other three, a little more serious, a little closer to each other. It was unusual to see Fitz angry, but pissing off Stratton would generally do the trick.

"What the hell, Barrett? You nervous for the meeting this weekend or something?"

Nervous? No.

Frustrated? Deprived? Lost in a loop of the memory of Emily climaxing against his hand on the tennis courts? Yes.

They had laid quietly with one another for a long time in the darkness before Emily sat up and fastened her bra, buttoned her shirt, and then stood to tuck it back into her jeans. He had looked up at her, at her blonde hair framing her face in the moonlight.

"I don't know what to say," she'd whispered.

He sat up. "How about . . . your rule is ridiculous?"

Her eyes had narrowed, but he kept talking like a total moron. "I *like* you, Emily. I *really* like you. It doesn't matter if you work for me. It doesn't matter if you call yourself my fake fiancée or my girlfr—"

She'd gasped, looking down at him with her hands on her hips. "Don't."

"Why not? That's what I want you to be."

She'd shaken her head, turning and walking quickly off the tennis courts. Barrett had sprinted after her, grabbing her elbow when he caught up to her.

"Stop! What?"

"I'm not your girlfriend. I can't be . . . yet. You need me to do a job for you this weekend, and I'm going to take money for it. That's real."

"Frankly, it doesn't get any more real than what just happened between us."

"That was just physical."

He'd winced. Because for him? What they'd just experienced together was *far* more than physical.

"Got it," he'd said, dropping her arm.

They walked the rest of the way back to the gatehouse in silence. When they got there, Emily turned to him under the oak tree, reaching for him. "I didn't mean it, Barrett."

"Which part?"

"It *wasn't* just physical."

He clenched his jaw, searching her eyes in the moonlight, then opened his arms to her, grateful when she stepped into them, laying her head on his shoulder.

"And that's what scares me," she continued. "I'm feeling things for you that need to wait at least another week. This is all happening really fast and the timing's bad and—" She swallowed, pulling away from him.

"My landlord raised my rent," she blurted out. "And we don't have that kind of money. I need to make some extra and this trip is the perfect way. It'll cover our rent for four or five months while we look for a new place."

"New place?" he asked.

"We can't stay there. It's too expensive." He had pulled her closer so she couldn't see his eyes and she rubbed her cheek against his shoulder, finally wrapping her arms around his waist. "I guess I sound pretty pathetic to someone like you."

His heart. Literally. Clutched.

He had never felt like such a crappy human being in his entire life. He'd done this to her. He'd made her feel this way. He'd forced her to think about moving. For a deal. For a goddamned deal. Was a deal more important than Emily? Was it worth risking her?

For ten years, his life had been all about being "the Shark," the dealmaker, the kingmaker. And now he stood in the moonlight with a beautiful woman in his arms, and he had to question what he wanted. He was perilously close to answering: Emily. Above all else.

Instead he took a deep breath and stroked her back. He'd change his ways after this deal. He'd never risk her again. "It doesn't sound pathetic. You'll come with me this weekend. I'll do the deal, you'll get your money, and then . . ."

She rotated her neck so that her lips faced his throat and sighed, her warm breath fanning his skin and making him hard again in an instant. "We'll see."

We'll see you in my bed, and I promise I will never, ever use you or deceive you like this ever again, Emily Edwards. I promise.

He leaned down and pressed his lips to hers, nodding. "We'll see."

Snapping out of his reverie, Barrett scowled at the Philadelphia skyline, feeling deprived and guilty. That was the last conversation they'd had before he kissed her good-night and five days later, he still felt like a total dirtbag for worrying her and making her think she needed to find a new apartment. He just wanted to get the weekend over with, and Sunday couldn't come fast enough. Barrett wouldn't rest easy until the Harrison deal was done, and Emily was his official girlfriend, and there were too many variables that could shake up his endgame between now and then.

So, to answer Fitz's question: Was he nervous about the weekend? "No. Not a bit."

Fitz rolled his eyes and clenched his jaw. He knew Barrett was lying, and Fitz never lied. He also never cheated, and he certainly wouldn't consider deceiving the woman he was falling in love with just to make a deal happen.

"Great. Then stop being an asshole." Fitz snapped the binder closed in his hands and headed out of Barrett's office without another word.

Barrett sighed. He'd see Emily tomorrow and in three short days, this entire fiasco would be over and they could be together for real. *Stick with the plan. It will be okay.*

"It will all be okay," he reassured himself, as though saying the words aloud would make them come true.

"I still can't believe you haven't seen him since Saturday night," said Valeria on Friday afternoon, sitting on Emily's bed in tights and a leotard as Emily packed for the Hamptons. "Because it sounds like your little rendezvous was pretty hot."

Valeria added the last part in a singsong voice that included her picking up Emily's thong undies and zinging them at her like a slingshot. Emily took them off her head, giving her roommate a look. "Very mature, Val."

"I am *dying* for details, and you won't give them up!"

"You know all you need to know. We made out a few times. I think we have real feelings for each other, but we're putting all of that on hold until we get back from the Hamptons."

"Because you're not a prostitute."

"Pretty much." Emily sighed. "Though I've had a weak moment a time or two this week."

"I can only imagine what'll happen when you're within touching distance."

Emily winced, then took a deep breath, folding her only sexy nightgown and tucking it into the suitcase.

"I mean, you *are* sharing a room, right?"

Emily nodded. "Presumably."

"Which means sharing a bed, right?" asked Valeria meaningfully. "Which means—"

"Which means maybe we'll bundle," said Emily quickly, watching Valeria's attention syphon to her favorite subject matter in an instant. Phew. Emily was hot and bothered enough about Barrett without discussing it further with her roommate. Not to mention, she wasn't entirely sure she was ready to think about sleeping with Barrett English. Sex wasn't something that had ever ranked very high on Emily's to-do list. Now faced with the opportunity to sleep with Barrett, she felt a little out of her depth.

"That's sort of a cool idea, Em. You know, it was a really important courting gesture in colonial America. It was the only way you could be intimate without being . . ."

"Intimate," Emily supplied. Early-American courting rituals were Valeria's department, but Emily had to admit, she found the material fascinating. Luckily, Valeria did too, because she laid off of Barrett and her quest for sordid details.

"Is *everything* off limits between you two? Because even though bundling precluded below-the-neck contact, and even though the two young people were supposed to talk all night—*yeah right*," she muttered disdainfully, "it's popular belief that most couples spent at least a portion of the night, you know, kissing."

"I know kissing," Emily muttered. "And I know what it leads to. I don't think it's a good idea, Val."

"Too bad." She sighed. "He's so hot and you're long overdue to see some action."

Emily gave her roommate an exasperated look. When Val wanted details, she was relentless. "Don't you have a class to teach? A mango or something?"

Val tapped her lips. "You either mean a mambo, which *Tia* Angelina does not teach, or a tango, which she does. Speaking of mambos, there's a horizontal version I bet Barrett wouldn't mind doing with you. You know, when you're ready."

"Gah! Do you think we could stop talking about it?" asked Emily, slipping into the bathroom for her toiletries and coming back out with a small fabric bag. "It's just making it harder."

"That's what he said," said Valeria, giggling. She sat up on the bed, cocking her head to the side when Emily didn't crack a smile. "Okay. I'll stop. Hey . . . in other news, I'm making headway on the new landlord, but it's really convoluted."

"How so?" asked Emily, distracted by which outfits to pack as Valeria rattled on behind her. Should she bring her blue suit and black dress? Probably for the evenings. But what would she wear during the day? She took out some ironed khaki pants and a navy blue cotton blouse. It wasn't fancy but the lines were clean. She found her dark, skinny leg jeans at the bottom of her drawer and packed them with an Irish cable-knit sweater her mother made for her on her eighteenth birthday. It had classic lines, and it was warm.

". . . so all I've been able to find out is that the building is now owned by a company called Giverny Holdings."

Emily's head snapped up. "What?"

"Giverny Holdings. Why? Does that mean anything to you?"

Emily shook her head. "Not really. My parents met in Giverny. That's all."

"Huh. So that's where your story begins, huh?"

"More or less, I guess." She shrugged. "That's the only reason it stood out to me."

"Well," said Valeria, "I'm going to find out where Giverny Holdings is registered and then I'm going to figure out who's behind it so I get the name of the person who owns this damned building . . . and *then*, I'm going to give them a piece of my mind."

"Don't burn bridges," warned Emily, zipping up her suitcase. "We can now afford to stay here until after New Year's with the money I'll be bringing home on Sunday."

"I have to get going." Valeria sighed, standing up to hug her friend. "Should I wish you luck?"

Emily sighed right back, pulling up the handle of her suitcase and rolling it to the door. "Wish me strength."

"Strength," said Valeria cheerfully as the apartment buzzer sounded to tell them Barrett had arrived.

It wasn't that she was dressed to the nines (she had on those soft jeans with a simple black sweater and her black slip-on shoes), or that she looked especially coiffed (her hair was back in a simple ponytail), or even that she'd flashed him a special smile (she hadn't). She kept her eyes downcast. But he had thirsted for a glimpse of her since Saturday and seeing her walk out the front door of her apartment building made his heart throb with yearning. Every part of his body longed for every part of hers, and it took every bit of his tattered self-control not to reach for her.

"Thank you for agreeing to do this," he said, opening her door as Smith put her suitcase in the trunk of the town car.

"Of course," she answered in that well-modulated tone she'd cultivated by living at Haverford Park for most of her life. "Thank you for inviting me, Barrett."

Once she was seated, he reached into his pocket and took out the engagement ring. "Ready for this?"

Instead of letting him put it on his finger, she held her palm flat and he dropped it onto her skin, neatly avoiding all contact. "As ready as I'll ever be."

Barrett started to raise the privacy window between the front and back seats, but Emily sidled closer to the window to say hello to Smith, so he lowered it again.

"How's tricks, Smith?"

"There's no such thing as a free lunch, Miss Emmy."

"Misery loves company."

"Count your blessings, child."

"Never put off until tomorrow what you can do today."

"All's well that ends well," he replied, chuckling softly. "You win."

"I always win," said Emily, cheeks pink and eyes bright when she turned back around to face Barrett.

"Let's go, Smith," said Barrett, raising the window. Emily scooted back to sit beside Barrett, leaving a foot of distance between them which he hated. He glanced at the glass behind which Smith was driving. "What on earth was that?"

"Me and Smith? We go way back. He used to let me help wash the cars on Sundays. It was a pretty fun time, let me tell you."

"Do you always speak to him like that? In clichés?"

"Know what's cliché, Barrett? The tone you're using right now." Her lips tightened and her eyes looked disappointed. "Smith is quick and smart. While you're at business meetings and when your flights are delayed, he's doing crosswords and other word games while he waits for you. We've been playing 'Cliché' since I was little. It made me feel smart . . . and important. I'd never let him down by refusing a round. It's how we say hello."

"I'm not judging you."

She shrugged, crossing her arms over her chest and looking out her window. "Feels like it a little."

"I'm not. I promise, Emily, I'm not. I think you're amazing."

"The amazing gardener's daughter."

"That's right," he answered evenly, refusing to rise to her bait, refusing to even acknowledge that she was anything except his equal in every way. He changed the subject. "I hated being away from you this week. I'm not fit for company."

"Well, you better get fit," she said. "We've got a long weekend ahead."

He clenched his jaw, looking out his window as he asked her quietly, "Did you miss me?"

She was silent for a long time and when he finally looked over at her, she was still staring out her window like the highway from downtown Philly to the airport was the most fascinating strip of space she'd ever seen.

"Yes," she finally whispered without moving, without looking at him, without giving anything else away.

He turned back to his window. It would have to be enough. For now.

The moment she saw him standing by the car door, blond hair burnished in the afternoon light, she knew staying away from him this weekend was going to be the battle of her life, which was precisely why she picked a quarrel with him. He hadn't done anything wrong, though his tone had adopted that haughty quality she'd always disliked when he asked about "Cliché." He did realize she was a child of the help, right? And that her parents and other English family employees, like Smith, were her equals, right?

She bit her bottom lip. She had worried about this from the very beginning. Would it be a problem for them?

She didn't need to think about the question for long before the answer came to her: No. No it wouldn't. For all of Barrett's privilege, and despite her previous worries, he really wasn't much of a snob.

Emily glanced at him as surreptitiously as possible, at his sharp suit and crisp tie. His long lashes reflected in the glass of the window. She thought about him dicing onion in her parent's kitchen and drinking Edwards' Select out of the bottle. The way he'd called a doctor to care for her mother and laughed good-naturedly during dinner with her father. The way he looked in jeans and a T-shirt, or the way he'd just asked if she missed him. Barrett could certainly act superior at times, but mostly in matters of business. For as far back as Emily could remember, regardless of the boundary that should have existed between them, Barrett had treated her as an equal. His feelings for her were genuine. Emily was sure of it.

Smith drove them to the hangars where the smaller, private planes took off, helping with their luggage and agreeing to meet them at 4:00 pm on Sunday in the same spot.

"Happy trails, Miss Em," he said, giving her a worried grin.

"Until we meet again," she crooned in response.

Without actually touching her, Barrett gestured to the waiting prop plane and Emily preceded him up the little stairs and into the tiny Robin 160A. There were two seats in the front for the pilot and co-pilot and two in the back for passengers.

"Hey, Jimmy," said Barrett, pulling the airplane door shut behind him and latching it. "Kip."

The two men looked up and smiled.

"This is Emily Edwards. She's my plus-one today to Easthampton."

Kip offered his hand. "Good to know you, Emily."

Emily smiled back politely and shook hands before taking the seat behind Kip. Jimmy already had his headphones on and gave her a slight wave from his seat, kitty-corner to hers. Instead of a proper ceiling, there was a bubble of greyish-brown glass over Emily's head which probably led to great views, but did nothing to assuage her fear of heights. She took a deep breath, trying to calm her pounding heart.

Barrett sat down beside her, clicking his seatbelt together. "Hey. You okay?"

"I've only flown a couple of times and never in a plane this small."

"Oh. Well, don't worry. Jimmy and Kip are pros. They've been flying me all over the country for years now."

She swallowed the lump in her throat as the propellers whirred louder. Barrett picked up some headphones hanging over the armrest of his seat and pointed to hers, then to her ears.

Emily nodded, putting the headphones on over her ears, but her fingers were trembling violently as she lowered them to the armrests of her seat. Her nails dug into the soft beige leather as they turned toward the runway, picking up speed. Just before the plane lifted off, she turned to Barrett with wide eyes and before she could process what he was doing, he leaned over the seat, and she felt his lips pressing against hers, his hands cradling her face, his fingers threaded into her hair. Utterly shocked by his actions, she leaned toward him, her own hands rising from the seat to cover his, to press them more firmly against her face, as she laced her fingers through his.

She shifted in her seat, leaning sideways to be closer to him, her stomach dropping as they gained altitude—or was it butterflies in her stomach from the touch of his tongue against hers? Whatever it was, it felt more comforting and more dangerous and distracting than the tiny plane that was almost in the clouds now.

Finally, Barrett pulled away from her, lips glistening, and mouthed, "Are you okay?"

She lowered her hands from his, nodding.

Reluctantly, he let his hands slip from her face, his smoky eyes holding hers as he returned them to his lap.

"Sorry," he mouthed, giving her a sheepish shrug.

"It's okay," she mouthed back, feeling grateful for the way he'd distracted her. It was as though he knew exactly what she'd needed and then offered it to her. More and more, that's who Barrett was in her life—the person who gave her what she needed. The person who called doctors in the middle of the night and helped her make extra money for her rent. The person she wanted beside her when tiny planes shook and rattled on takeoff.

And suddenly Sunday seemed a million years away.

Oh, Lord, she thought, her racing heart calming as she looked out the window at the little towns and villages that rushed past below, *please let this weekend fly by as fast as this little plane.*

Chapter 9

"Emily!" exclaimed Hélène, holding out her hands as Emily stepped into the foyer of the grandest home she'd ever seen, next to Haverford Park. The Harrison's Hamptons "cottage," Trade Winds, was a rambling grey-shingled mansion set at the end of a private lane with sweeping 180 degree views of the ocean. "You're finally here!"

Emily took Hélène's hands and allowed herself to be folded against the older woman's chest. "Your mother?"

"Much better, Mrs. Harrison."

"*C'est bon*! And you *must* call me Hélène! We're good friends now." She beamed at Emily, wrapping an arm around her waist and ushering her to the staircase. "But, you've also arrived at the worst possible moment! We're all headed out for an impromptu sail, though I know that you, and your adorable fiancé"—she leaned to the right to kiss Barrett's cheek—"can find *something* to do for the hour we're gone? *Oui?*"

"Oh, I . . ." Emily flushed, taking a deep breath and chuckling awkwardly at Hélène's innuendo.

"Josephina! Please take Mr. English and *Mademoiselle* Edwards up to their room! Cocktails on the dock in an hour!"

In a flurry of silk scarf and perfume, Hélène click-clacked through the house to catch up with the rest of the sailors.

Barrett looked at Emily, barely suppressing a grin, and Emily's shoulders shook lightly as she turned and followed Josephina-the-maid up the stairs. Hélène Harrison was certainly larger than life in her own digs.

They turned right at the landing, and then followed Josephina down to the end of the hall where she opened the last door on the left. She gestured for them to enter. "Your bags will be up in a moment."

"Thank you so much, Josephina," said Emily, smiling at the young woman. "You're very kind."

Taken aback, the maid beamed at Emily and nodded as she closed the door behind them.

"You're nice to everyone," said Barrett softly from where he stood between two of four French doors that looked out onto the water. Through white gauze curtains Emily could see the green lawn that led down to the water, the waves and blue sky, sailboats bobbing in the breeze. Frankly, she was happy to look anywhere that didn't include the queen-sized bed that dominated the small, but charming, guest bedroom.

"My mother always had favorites. You know, of your houseguests. The ones who were nicest to her."

Barrett grinned, crossing the room and sitting down in an easy chair situated by a fireplace. Emily suspected he'd chosen to sit there, and not on the bed, to make her more comfortable, and she was grateful for it.

She was achingly aware of him in such close quarters, replaying their kiss in the limo, on her father's kitchen counter, in the plane, and—*oh, God*—on the tennis courts.

"It's so warm in here," she said, leaning away from the door and heading to the windows. She separated the curtains and opened a set of French doors that led to a balcony with two chairs. "Come sit outside with me?"

He'd been watching her from his seat by the fire and sighed, a little disappointed maybe to leave the intimacy of the small room. He stood, shrugging out of his suit jacket, which made the muscles on his back ripple. Emily stared with unabashed admiration, whipping her glance away when he turned around, but damn it, he caught her and grinned.

"Want to see anything else?" he asked in a low voice, loosening his tie. Emily watched as he took it off, then unbuttoned the two top buttons of his dress shirt.

Her mouth went dry. Completely gorgeous Barrett English, who had given her an *al fresco* orgasm on Saturday night, was standing in front of a bed, in a bedroom they were sharing, undressing. She pressed cool hands to hot cheeks and turned back to the balcony. "N-no, thanks."

How in the hell was she going to make it through tonight if she couldn't even watch him take his tie off?

She plunked down in one of the two chairs miserably, looking out at the spectacular view, which was all but lost on her.

"I was just teasing," he said, sitting down in the chair beside her.

"Don't," she said, biting her lip, staring out at the water. "Please don't tease me. It's hard enough."

Her life felt stupid and silly and out-of-control suddenly. She was in a beautiful place with the man she'd always wanted, but she couldn't touch him, couldn't tell him how she felt, couldn't do anything but fist her fingers and practice every bit of self-control she'd ever mastered in her life.

"Hey," he said softly, brushing a strand of her hair behind her ear. "It's going to be a miserable weekend if we can't, you know . . ."

She turned to face him.

"Well, we can't, '*you know*,'" she said using air quotes. "It's off-limits."

He scoffed softly, looking out at the water before shaking his head. "That's not what I meant. If we can't, you know—talk, laugh, tease . . . be around each other."

"Oh." She felt her face soften. "I'm just nervous, I guess."

"Want to hear something crazy?" he asked, flicking his glance to her, and she nodded. "Me too."

"Barrett, 'the Shark,' English? Nervous about being alone with a girl? I don't believe it."

Well, at least my confession lightened the moment, he thought.

The tension in the room from the moment they'd arrived had been almost unbearable. A big, plush-looking bed . . . and an hour. He groaned inwardly, pushing aside fantasies of how he'd like to spend that hour and turned to her.

"Then you obviously haven't met this girl."

"I guess not. Tell me about her," she said, re-crossing her legs so they pointed at him.

"I'm not sure I should."

"Why not?"

"Well, I'm not allowed to like her this weekend. Not as much as I do, anyway."

"Is that right?"

He nodded, doing his best to look pathetic. "Liking her is 'off-limits.'" He used air quotes just as she had a few minutes ago.

"Hmm," she hummed. "But if you *were* allowed, what would you say captivated you about her? In the beginning?"

"In the *very* beginning? Her eyes."

Emily's lips twitched as her cheeks bloomed pink.

"I held her on my lap, and she stared up at me from her little pink blanket with the bluest eyes I'd ever seen, and . . ." His voice trailed off as he stared into those same blue eyes now.

"And?" she whispered.

He took a deep breath, letting his thoughts segue easily from images of the baby he'd held in his arms to memories of her as a little girl.

"When she was little she wore blonde braids everywhere she went. They trailed down her back and her mother would tie ribbons in them, the same color as whatever shirt or dress she was wearing."

"What else?" she asked, her eyes wide and surprised.

He shrugged, unfastening a silver cufflink and setting it on a small table between their chairs. Emily picked it up and twirled it between her fingers. He watched as his cufflink caught the light and for a second he was jealous of it—of a stupid piece of silver—because she'd reached for it so effortlessly.

"When she was about ten, my mother told me that she broke her arm falling out of an oak tree." He rolled his cuff up slowly, concentrating on the task, not daring to meet her eyes. If they were soft, or worse, languid, he wouldn't be able to stop himself from pulling her into his arms. "I was a freshman in college when it happened, and I had planned to come home that weekend anyway, but something made me pick up a stuffed bear from the campus bookstore. I left it by her back door with a note that said—"

"*No more breaking anything,*" she whispered. "I didn't know it was you."

He still didn't look up. He took a deep breath through his nose, savoring the bracing smell of brackish air on the cool breeze.

"What else?" she whispered.

He unfastened his other cufflink and set it carefully on the table, not waiting to see if she'd pick it up, because if she did he'd reach for her fingers so that she'd touch him instead of the metal which had pressed against his pulse all day.

"The summer I finished my MBA program, she was sixteen." She started to interrupt him so he continued quickly. "I was home for the Summer Party and she looked so grown up, I swear to God, I had to remind myself she was still a kid."

"You barely said hello to me."

Barrett started rolling his other cuff carefully, deliberately, chuckling softly. "I didn't trust myself. You looked twenty, but you weren't . . . and I admit I kind of hated Wes for following you around all afternoon and making you smile."

Her blue eyes were soft and warm as she looked back at him. "Will you hate me if I ask . . . what else?"

"I don't know how to hate you," he murmured.

Her breath caught, and he watched her wet her lips, her eyes beseeching. "Barrett. Please."

Watching her mouth made blood shoot to his groin in a rush. She was begging him to stop and yet begging him to go, and as much as he wanted to reach for her, he knew he shouldn't. He cleared his throat, returning his attention to his sleeve.

"When she was eighteen she went away to Paris—to Giverny—for the summer to stay with her aunt. At first I didn't know where she'd gone, but I summoned the courage to casually ask her mother where she was. When I learned she wouldn't be back until late-August, I considered buying a ticket and going to Paris for the weekend . . . just for a glimpse of her." He flicked a glance up to see the mesmerized look in her eyes, before looking back down again to push his sleeves to his elbows before sitting back in his chair and staring out at the sea. He shrugged. "But I had just made Vice President at English & Sons, so I couldn't pick up and go. I woke up every day thinking about it, though. I talked myself in and out of it a hundred separate times."

Emily was quiet beside him, her fingers still rolling the monogrammed cufflink as she breathed just loud enough for him to hear, for him to know how much his words were affecting her.

"What else?" she asked in a soft, hitched voice.

"When she was nineteen, I almost got engaged."

She gasped beside him and the cufflink fell from her fingers, clattering to the floor and skittering to the edge of the small balcony. She leaned down to pick it up, then placed it on the table beside its mate with trembling fingers.

When she looked at him, his breath caught from the confusion in her eyes. Possessive, furious, longing, uncertain, surprised. For him. Over him. He clenched his jaw because her face was telling him so much he wanted and needed to know about how she felt, even if she wasn't sure herself. It gave him hope—real hope that when Sunday rolled around they'd be together at last.

"I didn't know," she whispered.

"No one knew," he said. "I never asked her."

"What happened? You were twenty-seven . . ." She looked away from him, and he could almost see the cogs in her mind working to remember who he was dating when she was nineteen years old. "B-Bree . . ."

"Bree Ambler."

"Yes." Emily nodded, her brows furrowing. "She came for Boxing Day."

"My mother never approved of non-family for Christmas Day, but I wanted to re-introduce her to everyone before I popped the question, so I invited her for the day after." He clenched his jaw, unable to look at Emily anymore without reaching for her, touching her, tasting her. His nostrils flared and he stood, pressing his palms against the railing.

"What happened?" she asked from behind him, a tremor in her voice.

Barrett turned his eyes to her lovely, upturned face and said simply, "You were there."

You were there.

The words slammed through her like cyclone blast, knocking the wind from her chest and watering her eyes.

He shrugged, turning his back to the ocean so he faced her. "When I walked in with Bree, there you were. Long legs, blue eyes, blonde hair. I hadn't seen you in about a year, and you'd grown into an adult in that time. I couldn't take my eyes off you, and I knew it wouldn't be fair to go any further with Bree. I broke up with her that evening on the way back to the city." He swallowed, searching her eyes.

She felt her face contort in disbelief, and hope, and quiet agony for the situation they were in. Though she'd always loved Barrett in her own quiet way, Emily had been in the dark about the feelings he'd harbored for her for most of her life. To learn that he'd watched her, studied her, admired her for so many years? That he'd walked away from a possible wife because of her? It was almost too much to process all at once.

Emily stood up without saying a word and walked into the quiet of the bedroom, wanting to escape him, wanting to make love to him, having no idea how to handle the primitive beating of her heart that drummed for him and in fear of him. Her blood coursed through her veins with lust and warning, and her cheeks were so hot and flushed, it felt like July instead of October.

"Emily?"

He stood just inside the room, tall and strong in the doorway, his blue eyes dark with concern.

"Barrett," she warned him.

"You kept asking," he said in a low, unapologetic voice, rooted where he stood.

She bit her bottom lip.

"Don't," he growled.

Heat flushed the surface of her skin like a burn at the simple command. She released her bottom lip before slowly and deliberately grabbing it between her teeth again.

He crossed the room in an instant, holding her head between his hands as his lips descended upon hers urgently, passionately, punishingly, their teeth clanking together, their breath mingling in pants as their tongues sought one another madly. Emily plunged her fingers into his golden hair, which had been warmed by the sun outside, and moaned into his mouth as he pushed against her. She felt the bed behind her knees and let him push her just enough that she fell backwards, and he covered her body with his, his chest crushing her breasts as he plundered her mouth, demanding, stealing, taking everything she had to give after a lifetime of wanting. And she surrendered. She offered everything to this man who seemed so cold, but burned so hot, who made her forget everything that existed in life but him.

"Emily," he breathed, his lips grazing the tender skin of her jaw, pressing hot, wet kisses in a path to her ear, then taking the soft lobe between his teeth. She bucked against him from the sweet sharpness of the sensation, whimpering, clasping his face and redirecting his lips to hers.

That he should remember little details about her life so vividly, preserving them like treasures wrapped in tissue, humbled her, delighted her, devastated her. He was Barrett English and she was Emily Edwards. What did it mean that he should shadow her life so devotedly? Did it mean—could it possibly mean—that he was in love with her? The idea was so thrilling and yet so completely terrifying, she tore her mouth away from his, tilting her neck to the side so she couldn't see his eyes.

"Stop," she panted, dropping her hands from his face to rest them on the bed at her sides. "Stop. Please."

He sighed, long and deep, his hot breath making her shiver as his lips rested against the pulse in her neck. He made a strangled sound in his throat, as though he were going to try to say something, then thought better of it. The warm, heavy weight of his body still pressed intimately against her.

"Just give me a second," he murmured, his hands gradually sliding from her hair to the bed on either side of her head. He pushed down and his feet hit the ground at the foot of the bed.

As he stood, Emily twisted her neck and looked up at him from where she still lay on the bed, taking in his worried eyes and the frustrated set of his jaw. Looking away again, she sat up, the blood rushing to her head as she scooted to the foot of the bed. She kept her head down, which meant that she stared at his waist directly in front of her. She swallowed, letting her eyes drop to his hips, to the enormous bulge in his pants. She nearly whimpered, wishing they weren't bound by an agreement that included money, wishing they could explore all of the feelings between them that had been growing their whole lives and were finally coming to a head. It seemed that the feelings would not be put on hold, no matter how hard she tried. Perhaps because her heart—which would have needed time to adjust and expand to include a new love in her life—had already accommodated Barrett long ago.

"It's not that I don't want to," she murmured miserably, sitting on her hands so she wouldn't be tempted to reach out, to pull his body to her and rest her head on his flat, hard stomach.

"It's that you won't."

"It's that I *can't*," she said, finally looking up at him with glistening eyes and bruised lips.

He nodded, pursing his lips and she had a glimpse of boardroom Barrett, who didn't like taking no for an answer. He surprised her by offering a thin smile. "Have it your way, Emily."

He grabbed his jacket, turned on his heel and left the room.

Barrett had no idea where he was headed, but he certainly hoped his destination included a glass, some ice, and at least three fingers of decent scotch.

Damn it, but he hadn't meant to attack her like that. Well, he had. But, he hadn't. Did he want to sleep with her? Yes. Did every fiber of his being cry out for her? Yes. Had the past week been excruciating? Yes. But he hadn't started talking about his "Memories of Emily" as a seduction technique, he'd sort of fallen into it. And the more he remembered, the more he thought about their entwined lives, and the more sure he was of how much he needed and wanted her to be a permanent part of his future.

And that *damned* lip biting. What the hell was he supposed to do? He could make a strong case that she'd provoked him.

He turned left at the foot of the stairs and walked into a nautical-themed living room, beelining to the small wet bar sandwiched elegantly within the white bookcases. He took down a glass, uncorked a bottle of scotch, and poured himself half a tumbler.

"Drinking alone?"

Barrett spun in surprise. He hadn't noticed anyone else in the room, but he looked over at the windows to see J.J. Harrison's grey head peeking over the top of a wingback chair that faced a massive picture window looking out at the ocean.

"Sorry, sir," said Barrett. "I didn't see you there. I would have asked before pouring."

"*Mi casa es su casa*," said J.J., crossing the room to offer his hand to Barrett. His steel grey eyes assessed the younger man smoothly. "But my business is not your business . . . yet."

"You're not sailing, sir?"

"J.J., please. Let's pretend to be friends."

Barrett smiled wryly, dropping the older man's hand after a firm shake. He bet J.J. Harrison was quite the shark himself once upon a time. If they weren't on opposite sides of a deal right now, Barrett would openly admire his grit. "You're not sailing, *J.J.*?"

"I'm more of a fishing man. You?"

"Can't say I'm a huge fan of the water."

J.J. narrowed his eyes. "You're certainly a fan of my shipbuilding business."

"It's lucrative . . . or could be."

"It wasn't for sale," growled the older man.

"At least seventy percent of it was. We barely had to ask. Your brothers and sister want to sell."

J.J. huffed quietly, shaking his head. "Because they never worked a day in their lives at Harrison Shipbuilding, and it's all about squeezing it for every dime. Tough being the oldest, eh, Barrett? The whole family legacy falls to you."

Barrett took a long sip of his drink, his eyes carefully betraying nothing. No sympathy. No empathy. No connection. Business was business. Harrison Shipbuilding made yachts, cargo ships and fishing boats, and it made decent profits, but it was inefficiently run. Once in the hands of English & Sons it would be a genuine cash cow, and while Barrett actually did feel some small measure of sympathy for J.J. Harrison, he never let personal feelings cloud his business judgment . . . except, he thought bitterly, when dealing with Emily Edwards.

"A weak spot?" asked J.J., staring at Barrett thoughtfully.

Damn it. Stop thinking about her. "No sir. Excellent scotch. It has a little bite."

J.J. gestured to a framed photo on the bookcases beside the wet bar. It was black and white and showed a bearded fellow standing proudly beside a small fishing boat with the name "Trade Winds" neatly stenciled on the side.

"My grandfather built his first fishing boat with his own two hands. Such good craftsmanship, he built another and sold it, and then another. My father used to take me to the docks and point out the boats that my grandfather had handmade before they went into mass production. Now we sell yachts and cargo ships, too. But it all started with fishing boats made by hand. Don't you understand that?"

"It's a touching story. We know your heart is in Harrison Shipbuilding, J.J. And that's precisely why we'd like to offer you a position on the board and a guaranteed position as consultant for the next three years before we give you a very, very generous severance package."

"Screw you and your generous severance," growled J.J., taking an angry sip of his own scotch as he held Barrett's eyes. "Leave my company alone!"

"We've got seventy percent in the bag. I'll take over the board by Christmas, and we'll force you out if we have to."

Barrett stared at J.J. unflinchingly, waiting for that triumphant feeling to come over him . . . he'd felt it hundreds of times before and always compared it to the way he suspected early hunters must have felt when they delivered the death blow to their prey. Powerful, dominant.

Surprisingly, it didn't come today. For the first time in years, it didn't come. Barrett just felt bored and a little bad.

"Try it," snarled the older man. "My men will walk."

"Not at Christmas they won't." He knew all the things to say, but felt none of the pleasure saying them.

"I know the men who make these boats. I know the men who buy them. Can't you see that? Can't you understand?"

Barrett smelled her perfume before he saw or heard her walk into the room, and his voice softened, knowing she was near. "You've built a wonderful company, sir. We'll make it even better." Barrett didn't turn to face her, but the steel was all but gone from his voice when he finished by adding, "Take the deal, Harrison. It's in your best interest."

"We'll see, *Shark*," said J.J., searching Barrett's eyes mockingly before brightening his face with a smile. "Why, Emily, your timing couldn't be more perfect."

Chapter 10

It had been a long evening to say the least. From the moment Emily found Barrett and J.J. talking in the living room, Barrett had been in a pisser of a mood. There had been cocktails on the lawn followed by a lovely lobster dinner *al fresco* with a guitarist who strolled around the long candlelit table of eighteen guests taking requests. But with a taciturn Barrett to her left, obviously at odds with J.J. Harrison and probably still spoiling from their truncated make-out session, the evening had rolled on heavily. Emily mostly made polite conversation with the gentleman beside her, a fairly dull lawyer visiting from New York.

After dessert, when Emily was quite sure she'd learned everything possible to know about copyright law, she took her cue from three other guests who excused themselves for bed and did the same. As she stood, Barrett took her hand for the first time all evening, and after thanking Hélène and J.J. for a wonderful meal, he escorted Emily into the house.

She didn't wiggle her hand away because it felt so right and natural to be held by his and because she'd missed his warmth all night. Looking up at the tight set of his jaw as they ascended the stairs, it occurred to her that she had gotten so distracted by their attraction to each other, she wasn't doing a very good job of fulfilling her obligation to him. She was supposed to be his fiancée, someone who would smooth his rough edges and help him make the most of the weekend.

Emily laced her fingers through his, giving his hand a squeeze, fascinated to watch his jaw relax and the constricted lines of his face soften from the contact. It made her realize how much he needed her—to be a sounding board and a comfort. She'd offered neither of those things to him since he'd collected her this afternoon. She'd picked fights, needed him to reassure her on their airplane, and concentrated so much of their time in the room on his memories of her, she hadn't even asked about the deal he was here to pursue. She wasn't helping him, she was distracting him, all because her own heart was so affected by him.

Well, she could change things. What Barrett needed right now wasn't a love interest to make him all hot and bothered. What Barrett needed was the sort of woman who could be his friend. And when you love someone, you find out what they need, and you take pleasure in offering it to them the best you can . . . which is exactly what Emily intended to do.

He opened the door to their room, and she dropped his hand gently as they walked inside, determined not to let the intense sexual tension from the afternoon dominate the small space again. She looked at him in the dim light, turning on the lamp on the bedside table, then reached up to take off her earrings.

"Barrett," she asked, as he stood by the door. "Tell me what I walked into tonight when I interrupted you and J.J. Harrison."

He looked confused for a second, then rubbed his eyes with his fingers, and shrugged out of his jacket. Emily took it from him, walking it to the closet where she found a hanger and hung it up. When she turned around, he was sitting on the edge of the bed.

"I don't know what's wrong with me. My head's not in the game."

"What's the game?" she asked, slipping out of her heels and padding to the bathroom where she filled two crystal tumblers with water. She brought one to Barrett before sitting in the chair by the fire and facing him.

He looked at her, his face softening as he held the tumbler. "You can't possibly be interested in this."

"I promise you, I am."

He looked incredulous, but his lips tilted up. "Really?"

"You two looked like you were about to jump each other . . . and you've been quiet and brooding since."

"I definitely wanted to jump someone, but it wasn't J.J. Harrison." She flushed, shaking her head at him. "Flirt."

He sipped his water, staring at her from over the glass, as though deciding whether to push his advantage for more flirtation, or take her up on her offer to talk business. Finally, he sighed, pushing his shoes off his feet, and swinging his legs onto the bed. He lay back on the pillow, staring at the ceiling, and answered her question.

"I want to buy his company. He doesn't want to sell it."

"How can you buy something that's not for sale?"

"Well," he said, "he has three brothers and one sister who all own seventeen point five percent of the company each. That's seventy percent. None of them have ever worked for Harrison Shipbuilding or maintained an emotional connection to the company. They live off the interest from their shares, but otherwise have little to do with the day-to-day operations. Only one of them even serves on the board.

"Anyway, the company is valued at two hundred and fifty million dollars. Each of the siblings are lining up with their hands out for their forty-two million dollar shares. But, J.J. refuses to sell."

"At thirty percent, he'd make . . . oh my God, seventy-five million dollars? That can't be right!"

Barrett nodded at the ceiling. "It is."

"And he's *refusing*?"

"Yup. Digging his heels in, too."

"Why?"

Barrett sucked a deep breath through his nose and sighed. "He loves the company. He doesn't want to give it up. He doesn't want to relinquish control. Something about fishing boats and his grandfather."

"Ohhhh," said Emily. "He has an emotional investment in the company. I guess you can't put a dollar sign on that."

"Usually you can."

"So, what will you do? If he won't sell?"

Barrett huffed. "It'll get messy, but I'll still get the company in the end."

"How messy?"

"I'll buy the seventy percent. With that majority, I'll take over the board. I'll force him out."

"That sounds cold *and* messy," she observed, trying to keep the disappointment she felt out of her voice.

He flinched, which clutched at her heart, but she felt like maybe he should take a moment to think about what the company meant to J.J. Harrison.

"Cold or not, it *is* messy," he agreed, leaning up on an elbow and shifting to his side to look at her. "He has the loyalty of his employees. I could get a walkout at his factories. He could make things difficult for us. It wouldn't be the smooth transition I was hoping for."

"Isn't there another way?" she asked.

"If there is, I don't know what it is yet."

"You have to figure out what he wants. What would make him happy."

"Keeping his company. Not an option."

"You're smart, Barrett. Come up with another way."

She stifled a yawn, but stood, hoping to keep their conversation flowing as she changed into pajamas and arranged herself—wrapped up in a blanket, like bundling—beside him in bed. She unzipped her suitcase to look for her pajamas, only then remembering that all she brought was her only super sexy silk nightgown. She was trying to maintain this conversational vibe between them, and she knew that sexy pajamas would be distracting to Barrett.

"Shoot," she said. "I forgot my pajamas."

She glanced over at Barrett, realizing her mistake a second too late. His eyes widened, then darkened, as he stared at her. "No complaints here."

She pursed her lips, desperately trying to ignore how completely adorable he looked when he was flirting with her. "Can I borrow a T-shirt and some boxers?"

"You want to borrow my underwear?"

"I want something comfortable to wear to bed, Barrett. That's all."

His eyes raked deliberately down her body in the black cocktail dress she was wearing with bare feet. "What if I say no?"

"Then I'll sleep in jeans."

"And a bra?"

"And the shirt I wore today."

His lips twitched and he rolled his eyes, getting up from the bed to unzip his suitcase, which sat on a luggage rack across the room from hers.

"You know what, Emily? I hate your off-limits rules," he said, throwing her a clean pair of boxers and a T-shirt. "I really do."

She caught them against her chest and headed into the bathroom.

Me too, Barrett, she thought, as she changed. *Me too.*

While Emily changed in the bathroom, Barrett refused to think about her putting her naked body into his underwear, and forced his thoughts back to their conversation. It was no small feat. When she'd said, *I forgot my pajamas*, he'd gotten instantly hard. She hadn't even said it flirtatiously or as an invitation. Her tone had been matter-of-fact. God, he was losing his mind.

He rolled onto his back, pillowing his hands under his head. Dragging his body away from hers this afternoon had taken all of the strength he possessed and frankly, he was starting to wonder if it was a good idea to have Emily here at all. He couldn't have her. Thoughts of her were messing with his head so much that he couldn't even focus on business.

And yet. Having her here—in any capacity—felt so right to his heart, he needed to figure out how to still do business with Emily as a distraction. He wasn't getting rid of either in his life.

He glanced up when she came out of the bathroom. His T-shirt billowed over her chest, tucked into his boxers which were pulled up under her breasts. Her face had been scrubbed clean of makeup, she wore rimless glasses and her long, white legs and little feet padded softly around the bed. Did she look conventionally sexy? No. Had Barrett ever wanted anyone as much as he wanted Emily Edwards in that moment? No.

He groaned lightly as she pulled at the comforter and slipped into bed beside him, laying her head back on the pillow and sighing. Even though he was on top of the covers and she was under them, he was achingly aware of her proximity, and all he wanted to do was reach for her.

Rolling onto his side, he reached his arm out, draping it over her stomach. "Is this okay?"

She hesitated, her eyes searching his. "Can we be friends tonight?"

"*Just* friends?"

"I don't think we'll ever be *just friends*, Barrett. But can we try? Just for tonight?" she asked softly.

He sensed room for negotiation, but instead of pressing his advantage, he nodded, settling his cheek on the pillow beside hers, close to her shoulder. He pulled her a little tighter up against him, and she relaxed next to his body. It was uncharacteristic of him to back away from improving a deal, but Emily was shaking up everything he knew about who he was.

"We can."

"And a good friend listens . . . so keep talking," she said, snuggling deeper into the bed and closer to him, sighing in comfort.

Could he do this? Could he hold the woman he loved in a bed, in his arms, and just talk to her? He gazed at her face in profile, at the face he'd sought so many times throughout his life. If that's what she wanted, what she needed, then yes, he could.

"Well, I don't want a messy corporate transition. I prefer neat."

"I remember," she said, and he heard the laughter in her voice. She turned to him. "Your proposition? That day at Penn when you asked me to be your fake fiancée? You said, 'I don't want messy. I prefer neat.' Remember?"

He grinned at her, then pursed his lips and shook his head. "Ironic, huh? Because this is as messy as it gets."

"It's not," she insisted softly. "It's just temporary."

His smile turned to a frown, and he felt the lines of his face harden. "I don't want it to be temporary, Emily."

"*This,*" she said. "This *now*. You on top of the covers and me beneath them. It's just temporary."

His breath hitched as he understood her meaning. She was saying that them being apart was temporary? "But I thought you said, 'We'll see,' . . . after this weekend was over."

"Barrett," she whispered, rolling to her side and reaching up to cradle his cheek in her palm as their breath mingled in the valley of pillow between them. "I know what I want when this weekend is over."

"Me?" he breathed.

"You," she answered, leaning forward to brush her lips softly against his.

His heart shuddered with love for her, as his mind processed the fact that by not pushing her to negotiate, he'd somehow gotten exactly what he wanted. His fingers, which had flexed to clasp her to him through the covers, relaxed, though his arm still lay across her body, pulling her gently closer, though there was nowhere else to go.

She leaned back, her blue eyes bright and happy, as she smiled at him from mere inches away. "And you want me."

"Always," he answered solemnly, swallowing the lump in his throat as he drank in the beauty of her face, the wisps of hair that lay soft and flat against her ear, the light eyelashes that fluttered delicately behind glasses, the freckles that dotted her nose, the pink softness of her lips. He'd told the truth: he was solidly and irrevocably in love with her and he always had been.

"Now tell me more about the deal."

Emily saw it in his eyes, the intense way he watched her without fighting what was happening between them. He loved her. She was sure of it.

She withdrew her hand from his face, pillowing them both under her head as she stared at him, giving him a small, encouraging smile.

He sort of mentally shrugged. "Not much else to say."

"There is more. I know it. I can feel it."

"Okay." He sighed. "Doing a deal usually feels good. Really good. Like skiing down a mountain, or jumping from a plane, or great sex. It's exciting. It's a rush. But, this doesn't feel exhilarating . . . and I can't put my finger on why."

Great sex. Huh. Emily got stuck as the words circled around in her brain. Great sex. Hm. How many people had Barrett enjoyed great sex with? How great was the great sex he'd experienced? How would the sex they had compare to the great sex he'd had with other people? Would it even be great at all?

With four years spent in undergraduate school, another three totally focused on her masters, and now another deeply entrenched in doctoral studies, there hadn't been much time for boyfriends. It's not that Emily wanted to be a twenty-four-year-old virgin, and she certainly wasn't opposed to sex or afraid of it, but she'd never quite gotten around to . . . well, *having* it. She'd always *meant* to give it a try—find someone suitable, date for a while, fall in love, and have the "great sex" moment. It just hadn't happened . . . yet. Furthermore, she'd never allowed her sexual status—*or lack thereof,* she thought dryly—to define who she was. No, she hadn't had sex yet. Yes, she liked lemon yogurt. They were parts of who she was, neither sum nor total.

But, now, hearing Barrett glibly mention "great sex" as a matter of course, she couldn't help but wonder . . . would she disappoint him? Would he disappoint her? Would it bother him that she'd read a lot of books, and even watched a couple of dirty videos, but she hadn't actually done the deed? Great sex probably came from having a really experienced partner, huh? And she wasn't. She was—

"Emily?" he asked, and she suspected it was the second time he'd said her name.

"Mm-hm?"

"Are you still listening?"

"Of course."

"So, I'm not feeling that rush this time . . . I mean—"

"Um," she interrupted. "How great?"

"What?"

"The, um, the great sex you mentioned. How great?"

His mouth dropped open and he stared at her, a smile tilting his lips up in surprise.

"You said . . . 'Like skiing down a mountain, or jumping from a plane, or great sex.' And I was just wondering, um, how *great* is great?"

If possible, his eyes opened wider.

She scrunched up her nose and winced. She was making herself look like a complete idiot. Her neck flushed hot, and she knew she was turning pink.

"Uh, just forget I asked."

"I can't really just forget that, Emily."

"Please try."

"Emily." He chuckled, reaching for her face and nudging it to look at him. "What's going on? Do you really want me to . . . I mean, do you want details or—?"

"No! No. It doesn't matter. Tell me more about the deal . . . you're not getting a rush . . ." she prompted.

His eyebrows furrowed. "You know, I'm not Alex. It's not like I've been a total manwhore, if that's what you're implying."

Her eyes cut to his with precision, and she knew he could see the hurt behind them. Manwhore or not, she didn't want to know how many women Barrett had been with. She couldn't bear it. It hurt her to even consider it.

"I'm not implying anything. Forget it. Please, Barrett."

"I mean it's not like either of us are virgins."

She cleared her throat and cast her eyes down, squeaking out an awkward, "Mm-hm."

She felt him staring at her, searching her face. When she couldn't bear it anymore, she flicked her eyes up and caught his smile fading like he was looking at something unbelievable or impossible. Her whole body tingled with the uncomfortable feeling of being found out. She'd never felt so transparent.

"Emily," he said slowly, almost reverently. "That's not possible."

She gulped softly, wetting her lips with her tongue, as she looked down again.

It was nothing to be ashamed of, she reminded herself. It's not like she hadn't dated men. She had. Quite a lot, in fact. She'd just never really been in love enough with any one of them to consider sleeping with them. It wasn't a big deal. Or it certainly hadn't felt like a big deal to her . . . until now.

She lifted her chin and met his eyes. "It's not a big deal to me."

His face froze, and she couldn't read his expression, but it wasn't comfortable or even remotely reassuring. It waffled between disbelief and shock, and she couldn't handle it much longer. For all of the comfort that had built up between them over the last week, over the last few months of "fake dating," over a lifetime of watching one another from across the wide lawns at Haverford Park, she'd never felt further from Barrett than she did right this minute. And it felt awful.

"It's a very big deal," he finally murmured. "You've never . . . ?"

She shook her head.

He stared at her for one more tense moment, then rolled over onto his back, running his hands through his hair.

Emily was a virgin.

The idea was so hot and yet so terrifying, he didn't even know what to do with himself. The possibility that he could want her for his whole life, and end up being the first man to ever have her, humbled him to the point of speechlessness, and Barrett was not a man flummoxed by much.

He never would have guessed. From the way they'd made out in the back of the limo and at her house, and on the tennis courts—*Christ!*—there's no way he would have ever known. Her body was made for touching, made for loving, her responsiveness so sharp, it made him harden just remembering. If he wanted her badly five minutes ago, his lust for her now had tripled.

He tried to breathe normally, but her soft, supple, never-invaded body was warm under the sheets beside him, and he couldn't think about anything else but how much he wanted to be her first.

"Um, well, maybe it's time for sleep . . ."

Barrett heard the tremor in her voice, and leaned on his elbow to face her. Her face was uncertain and worried. She shrugged lightly, her eyes glistening as she stared at the ceiling.

"Hey. Hey, hey, hey. What's going on here?" he asked gently.

She dragged a knuckle over one brimming eye. "I'm weird, I know. It just never happened. I mean, I just . . . I never met the guy I wanted to—"

"Emily, stop. Wait. Stop," he whispered again, placing his hand on the covers over her stomach, right below her breasts. "Do you think I'm upset about this?"

"You seem upset. You seem freaked out."

He reached up with both hands to cup her cheeks, cradling her face, trying not to breathe too hard, but failing, because she was that precious to him, that perfect.

"I'm not freaked out, baby. I'm in awe."

As the words left his lips, his face softened to a look so tender and yet so passionate, so fiercely possessive, it took her breath away.

"You are?"

"I am."

"You're not weirded out?"

He shook his head, still staring at her with that same loving look that was shattering every barrier left between them.

Emily's heart, which had been thumping in embarrassment and isolation a moment before, picked up pace as his thumb swiped gently over her cheek to whisk away one, last errant tear.

"Sunday," she said softly, staring at his beautiful face, just inches away from hers. "Okay?"

"Okay," he agreed, lowering his elbow to rest his cheek on the pillow beside her, draping his arm back across her and pulling her as close as possible.

"Good night, Barrett English," she whispered, her heart too full for any more talking, any more revelations, any more feelings or discoveries.

"Good night, Emily Edwards," he whispered back, as if he knew it was time to stop talking, to let everything light and heavy between them settle into their hearts and minds as they dreamed.

He pulled her face to his until their foreheads touched, then they closed their eyes, and slept.

Chapter 11

The first thing Barrett saw when he woke up was Emily, her face mere inches from his, her breath surprisingly sweet for morning, her chest rising and falling in deep sleep. His arm lay heavy and limp over her hip, caught in covers, curled under her. Sun filtered into their room, highlighting her light hair like a halo and bathing her pale skin in warmth. She was an angel, a vision, and she was lying next to him. The revelations about her sexuality aside, the words that meant the most to him last night were these: *I know what I want when this weekend is over.*

Emily Edwards wanted him.

For as much as Barrett ruled a board room like a kingdom, buying and selling billion dollar companies with the flick of his wrist or a nod of his head, women had never actually been his forte. He'd never wanted for female companionship, of course, but his serious romantic relationships could be counted on one hand. They were always complicated by the image of a much younger woman lingering in the back of his mind.

He rolled onto his back, then swung his legs over the bed. He'd slept in his dress shirt and suit pants, not daring to move after pulling her head to his and hearing her soft, deep breathing soon after. It would have taken a natural disaster for him to budge.

As much as he'd like to stare at Emily all morning, the reality was that he had a deal to close and the best way to clear his head would be to take a morning run. He rummaged through his suitcase quietly, changed into navy shorts and a long-sleeved running shirt, pulling on his shoes and socks in the chair by the fireplace.

He looked back over at Sleeping Beauty, and he didn't want to wake her, but he didn't want to leave her either. He made his way softly to her side of the bed and squatted down until his nose was level with hers.

"Em," he whispered. "Emmy Faith."

She inhaled deeply, her eyes still closed and her voice low and sleepy. "Barrett?"

"I'm going for a run."

"Hmm," she murmured.

He leaned forward and pressed his lips against hers, which parted softly as a low, breathy moan escaped her throat. "Barrett."

"I'll be back," he whispered, nuzzling her nose before drawing back and standing up.

Leaving her was hell.

Thank God tomorrow was Sunday.

"So?" demanded Valeria. "More details about Operation Bundle, please!"

Emily tilted her head and wedged the phone between her ear and shoulder so she could brush her teeth.

"I can' lie. I's hard."

"Are you brushing your teeth while we're on the phone? You're disgusting, Emily."

Emily spat with gusto, then grinned at her reflection.

"You love me. You know it."

"I don't think I'm the only one."

"Val! He hasn't come remotely close to sharing that feeling."

"Who are you kidding? Recounting your childhood and adolescence like that? Falling asleep with his forehead pressed against yours, fully dressed? He's not just interested in burning a hole in your panties. He likes you. He *really* likes you."

"I *really* like him," said Emily, pulling her skinny jeans and cable-knit sweater out of her suitcase. On today's agenda? A yacht ride with lunch. And though it was sunny, it would also be a high of fifty-eight degrees on the water. Chilly.

"Hey Em, did you tell him about your *special* status?"

"God, you make me sound like I belong in quarantine."

"No, no," said Valeria lightly. "I just, you know, I care about you."

"It doesn't mean anything," insisted Emily. She was getting sick of saying it. "I drink Earl Grey. My hair's blonde. I haven't had sex yet. I'm a doctoral student. It's no more or less important than any other fact about my life."

"You really believe that?" asked Valeria gently.

"I *really* believe that, and I refuse to make it a bigger deal out of it. I'm not scared. I'm not nervous. I'm twenty-four years old, and I have deep feelings for Barrett. If anything, I'm just plain ready. So, enough!"

"Okay, okay!" said Valeria, washing her hands of that part of the conversation. "So where's Prince Charming now?"

"No idea. I woke up and he was gone. His suitcase is still here, though. He didn't abandon me."

"What's the plan, Em?"

Emily buttoned her jeans then wiggled into her bra, balancing her phone against her shoulder again as she clasped it. Suddenly, strong, warm hands covered hers, and she pulled away as Barrett finished her work.

"I have to go, Val," she murmured, her skin flushing. She hadn't heard him enter the room. His hands ran slowly down her sides, finally resting on the skin of her waist.

She lowered her iPhone and pressed *End*, turning to face a sweaty Barrett. His hands skimmed her waist as she spun, then rested on her hips, his fingers splayed out and slightly grasping.

"Morning," he said, grinning at her.

"Not *good* morning?" she asked, tilting her head to the side and grinning back.

"*Good* would have been helping you get undressed instead of dressed." He shrugged and his eyes twinkled as they dipped to her breasts. "Or walking in twenty seconds sooner."

"Where were you?"

"Running."

"You better hurry, husband-to-be," she said, wiggling out of his arms. "We're expected on a yacht in twenty minutes."

He grabbed her waist again, pulling her up against his chest, his eyes searing as they caught hers. "Husband-to-be?"

"Just getting into character," she said, lacing her hands behind his damp neck with a happy shrug. "Last full day of playing fiancée for you. I wonder if I'll miss it."

"Maybe you won't have to."

Her mouth dropped open softly, and he took advantage, leaning forward to kiss her, his lips touching down gently on hers. She rose on tiptoes to meet him, stretching as he lifted her closer and touched his tongue to hers, setting off sparks in her brain. His arms encircled her and she sighed into his mouth, barely remembering what life looked like before last weekend when their "engagement" story made her see Barrett in a whole new light.

She kissed his lips softly one last time, then pulled back, but he didn't let go.

"You're getting me all sweaty," she said.

"Maybe you should come shower with me."

"Barrett!" she exclaimed. "My husband-to-be is so forward."

"My wife-to-be is so hot," he retorted, dropping his lips to her neck. She tilted it to the side to give him better access.

"Where has all this charm been hiding?"

"It hasn't been hiding," he said, peppering her throat with kisses, his voice deep and drugged. "It's been waiting."

"Oh, Barrett." She sighed, arching into him. "You're making this so hard."

"I think that's my line."

She chuckled, and it was a sexy, throaty laugh that sounded foreign in her ears.

"Maybe make it a cold shower," she suggested, pushing at his chest.

"You're killing me, woman," he said, backing away from her with a long sigh. She heard the shower turn on, so it surprised her when he peeked out of the bathroom door, bare chested. "Sure you won't join me?"

She couldn't lift her eyes from his chest. It's like they were somehow glued to the tan, toned contours of the hard body that he hid under his elegant dress shirts and Armani suits.

"Oh," she whimpered.

It was his turn to offer her the deep rumble of his laughter. "Breathe, Emmy."

"Okay," she murmured, taking a deep breath, but still staring, transfixed. Her fingers twitched at her sides, and she fisted them to keep from crossing the room and running them over his muscles.

He chuckled again. "Finish getting dressed."

Then he disappeared into the bathroom and Emily sank onto the bed behind her, repeating, *tomorrow, tomorrow, tomorrow,* in a whispered litany.

Barrett held Emily's hand as they made their way down the stairs and across the lawn to the yacht that waited at the Harrisons' dock. With her fingers laced through his, he felt on top of the world. The only thing nagging at him was that J.J. Harrison still hadn't agreed to sell, and Barrett was running out of time to make this a more peaceful transition.

Isn't there another way? Emily's voice bounced around in his head, but he couldn't think of anything. He specialized in corporate takeovers, not creative acquisitions. He wondered if he should call

Stratton and see if his younger brother had any suggestions, but that made him purse his lips. He was Barrett English. He didn't need to ask for help. J.J. Harrison needed to see reason and sign over his thirty percent. Barrett would make it happen by the end of today.

Hélène greeted them at the dock.

"No business on the boat, Barrett!" she said, waggling her finger at him. "I don't want to be responsible for you being thrown overboard!"

Barrett smiled politely, but when Emily giggled beside him, his smile widened into something more genuine.

"She's so good for you," observed Hélène, smiling at them both as she ushered them onto the main deck of the small ocean liner. "You will remember everyone from last night, and we have two more charming additions . . . my dear friend, Charity Atwell, and her daughter—"

Barrett's eyes widened to saucers as he shot a worried glance to Emily by his side.

Hélène moved slightly to the side and a beautiful, blonde woman turned to greet them, bursting into a beaming smile. "Barrett!"

"Fu . . . Felicity."

Barrett's hand was practically wrenched away from Emily's as Felicity threw herself into his arms, locking her hands around his neck.

"It's been months!"

"It has," he said, patting her on the back awkwardly and detangling her hands from his neck so he could pull away.

Felicity Atwell was beautiful, cultivated, and charming, and the Atwell family was one of the oldest in Philly. Though the Atwells and Englishes weren't particularly close, Barrett and Felicity had known one another throughout their adolescence, attending the same ball-room dancing school, playing tennis in the same intra-country club division, and sharing many of the same friends. At U Penn, they had several classes together, and though Felicity's blonde, blue-eyed prettiness appealed to Barrett, he'd never been particularly interested in her. He'd been far too focused on his studies, and had no interest in a steady college girlfriend.

After he and Bree Ambler had broken up a few years ago, he'd run into Felicity at a hospital benefit and asked her to dance. They'd ended up back at her apartment having decent, but unimaginative sex, and he'd taken her out for brunch the next morning to be a gentleman. He hadn't really intended to call her again, but it seemed like whenever they ran into each other, they'd end up sleeping together, and eventually it turned into a habit. When either of them was lonely or between significant others, they'd reach out, and if the other was free too, they'd make time to get together.

The problem was, the sex had never been better than decent, and the conversation had always circled back to their common backgrounds, as though Felicity were making a play for them to start dating. It made Barrett uncomfortable, and he'd called her less and less over the past year. But, it was only when he reconnected with Emily in May and started seeing her more regularly that Barrett realized Felicity's blonde-haired, blue-eyed looks were just an available substitute for the girl he really wanted. After that, he hadn't called her again.

"What good luck," she purred, releasing him. "We'll have to *get together* later."

Barrett shot a quick look at Emily, who was watching the proceedings with a mix of surprise and amusement, and took her hand, lacing his fingers through hers before she could pull away.

"Of course you know Barrett's fiancée, Emily Edwards?" asked Hélène cheerfully, putting her arm around Emily. "You must have all known one another at Penn! *Oui*? Where's your lovely mother?"

Hélène trundled off to find Charity Atwell, leaving the three younger people alone.

"Barrett's fiancée!" Felicity started laughing right away, a high-pitched tinkling sound that slowly ebbed off as she looked back and forth between Barrett and Emily with widening eyes. She gasped quietly, her lips still tilted up in latent amusement as her eyebrows knitted in confusion. Finally her amusement faded entirely and she clasped her hands delicately in front of her. "Fiancée?"

Barrett gritted his teeth for the most awkward introduction he'd ever had to make. "Emily Edwards, this is Felicity Atwell, an old friend. Felicity, this is my fiancée, Emily Edwards."

Felicity's devastated gaze didn't flicker from Barrett's eyes. "Your *fiancée*?"

Barrett nodded slowly, pulling Emily against his side. She held out her right hand to Felicity, and Felicity slowly allowed her eyes to drift to Emily. Barrett watched as Felicity swept her gaze over Emily's body, taking in her jeans and sweater, her blonde hair held back in a ponytail and the small gold studs in her ears. He could tell she felt superior to Emily, confident even, until her glance flicked to their bound hands, and the four-carat Harry Winston princess cut diamond engagement ring on Emily's finger.

Her eyes jerked back to Barrett's, and her mouth flew open. She placed a hand over her mouth and composed herself quickly. "I had no idea."

"It all happened very fast," answered Barrett.

"I'm sure it did," said Felicity, shooting daggers at Barrett before turning back to Emily. "What did you say your last name was?"

"Edwards," replied Emily, still holding out her free hand to Felicity.

"Emily Edwards. Hmm. I don't believe we've met," said Felicity, shaking Emily's hand quickly before pulling hers away.

"I was at Penn years after you."

Felicity flinched at the implication that she was much older than Emily and Barrett almost grinned, except he knew Felicity was probably hurt, and as much as he'd never had any serious interest in her, he wasn't anxious to hurt her either.

"A younger woman, Barrett," she said, her voice flirtatious, but her eyes hard.

"We've known each other forever," said Emily, and Barrett squeezed her hand gently at the nervous tremor in her voice.

"Is that so?" asked Felicity smoothly. A waiter walked by with a tray of champagne and Felicity took a glass. Emily shook her head no. "Well, what a coincidence, because I feel like I've known Barrett forever too . . . *intimately*."

Barrett clenched his jaw, stealing a quick look at Emily. If Felicity's insinuation bothered her, she didn't let it show.

"Barrett's a wonderful man," replied Emily smoothly. "How lucky for you to have known him in *any* capacity."

She was so dignified and yet so direct, her tone gentle and firm at once, he admired her. He was amazed and proud to see her holding her own.

"I just can't believe we never met," said Felicity, cocking her head to the side, desperately trying to place Emily as the younger sister of one of their society friends. "Are you the youngest?"

"The only," she answered.

"And you grew up in Haverford."

"I did. My parents are still there."

Felicity smiled thinly. She knew it was impolite to continue that line of questioning so she switched gears. The boat lurched softly as they cleared the dock and started for the open sea. Barrett wished he could take Emily upstairs to the viewing deck. Frankly, he wished he could take her anywhere that didn't include Felicity.

"So, Emily, what is it you do?"

"I'm a doctoral student at Penn."

"A student. How interesting." She said this like mud was far more captivating. "Your course of study?"

"Early American industrialization."

"Fascinating. And you went to U Penn undergrad like me and Bee."

"Yes, I did."

"How divine! Where did you pledge?"

"Pledge?"

"Tri-Delt? Chi-Oh?"

"Oh." Emily cleared her throat and shook her head. "No, I wasn't in a sorority. Though I was Phi Beta Kappa."

"Of course you were." Felicity's nostrils flared delicately as she smiled at Emily. Emily hadn't joined one of the social clubs offered on campus—she'd mentioned the club that only took the smartest students at Penn with the highest GPAs. Felicity Atwell had never come close to Phi Beta Kappa. "We should play a round of nine sometime. Get to know one another now that we have Barrett in common."

"I don't golf," said Emily, and for the first time, Barrett sensed a warning in her tone. She didn't like it that Felicity kept harping on her erstwhile relationship with Barrett and he understood. And he'd never admit it, but on some level he liked that she cared enough to be jealous.

"How's your tennis game?" asked Felicity.

Before the claws really came out, Barrett intervened. Emily had held her own like a champion, but it was time to put Felicity in her place, and he knew the best way to do it.

"She's dynamite on the tennis court," said Barrett gently in a low, suggestive voice, letting go of Emily's hand and shifting to put his arms around her waist from behind and pull her up against his chest. He felt her relax into him almost immediately.

"Honestly, I'm not very good at tennis, Felicity," Emily said, thankful Barrett had finally made a decisive move to establish which of them he belonged to. He leaned forward and rubbed his nose softly under her ear, and Emily forced her eyes not to flutter closed from the sweetness of the sensation.

As Felicity stared at them with unmasked fascination, her face fell—very subtly and quietly—and Emily felt an unexpected surge of sympathy for her. She could imagine, for a moment, how terrible it would feel to lose Barrett.

Emily knew about Felicity Atwell, of course. Barrett and Felicity appeared together regularly in the society pages, and they were the paper's favorite on-again, off-again couple. According to Smith—and even to Barrett—they'd never been in a committed relationship, but they'd certainly spent time together.

It didn't hurt Emily that Felicity existed. Or that's what she told herself. And rationally, it really didn't. Of course Barrett had been with other women. He was a young, vital man with needs, and Felicity had met those needs. Sure, it stung a little to imagine them together, but Emily worked hard to push those images from her mind. His arm was around *her* waist. And from everything he'd shared with Emily, *she* was the person he wanted in his life.

She tilted her head to the side, and gave Felicity a small smile of sympathy.

"Will you excuse me?" Felicity asked with glistening eyes, turning away from them and heading down a wood-paneled corridor.

Emily turned in Barrett's arms, sighing as she shook her head back and forth. "You didn't have to do that."

"I didn't like the way she was talking to you. Implying that you weren't our kind."

"I'm *not* your kind, Barrett."

"You're the only kind I want," he answered, pulling her closer, until her chin rested on his shoulder. "It doesn't bother you? Me and Felicity?"

"Do you have feelings for her?"

"No," he answered simply.

"Did you ever?"

"No. Not really."

"Do you have feelings for me?"

"You know I do. I'm crazy about you, Emily. I always have been."

She swallowed the lump in her throat that rose at the tenderness of his words.

"Then it's all okay," she whispered, leaning her cheek against his shoulder, perilously close to glistening eyes herself as he tightened his arms around her.

"I don't know if it's *all* okay. I hate to say it, but this is a bit of a snag, Emily. She'll tell everyone, you know," he said softly near her ear, "that you're my fiancée. It's only a matter of time until the whole world knows."

Emily drew back, brows creased and worried, as she searched his face. He was telling the truth. "My parents."

"I'll get ahead of it, okay? We're all trapped out on a boat in the Hamptons for now. She can't do much. I'll talk to Felicity. Let her know we're keeping it quiet, and ask her to respect that." She must have still looked worried, because he reached up to caress her cheek and she leaned into his touch. "Don't worry. I'll figure out a way to fix it."

"I trust you, Barrett," she said, closing her eyes and tilting her head to kiss his palm.

"I won't let you down," he said, his eyes full of tenderness as he watched her lips press against his skin. "I promise, Emily."

She smiled, and he dropped his mouth to hers, brushing his lips against hers with aching gentleness, before pulling her toward the stairs that led to the upper deck.

Chapter 12

Convinced that Emily would be well looked-after, flanked by Hélène Harrison and another older lady as the butlers cleared away the lunch dishes, Barrett followed J.J. Harrison to the bridge to finish their conversation about Harrison Shipbuilding.

As J.J. put on a white captain's cap and dismissed the ancillary crew, he gestured to the co-captain's seat, inviting Barrett to sit down.

"Are we in good hands with you at the helm, sir?" Barrett asked lightly.

"I'm not a hack, English. Unlike my brothers and sister who haven't set foot on a boat since they were in diapers, I try not to go more than a day or so without being on one. I know more about boats and boatbuilding than I do about anything else. It's why my father left me his share of Harrison Shipbuilding."

"Again, sir, that's the very reason we'd like for you to remain on the board."

"Let's cut the crap. You want me on the board so it looks like a peaceful transition."

"A peaceful transition wouldn't hurt the deal, that's true."

"As if you deserve my help," he huffed, hands on the traditional ship boat wheel, grey eyes staring out at the calm blue sea ahead.

"It's going to happen, Harrison," said Barrett gently, but firmly. "Whether you like it or not, we're going to buy your company. We're going to try to keep it together, and make it more profitable. If that fails to happen, we'll sell it off in parts. That's reality. Your choices are limited, but you do have choices."

Barrett knew the emotional implications of what he was saying. J.J. looked at Harrison Shipbuilding as other men looked at their children. The threat of separating the divisions would be the hardest pill to swallow.

"Carve up my father's company like a Thanksgiving turkey," he snarled.

Barrett cracked his knuckles before opening the door of the trap. 3-2-1 . . .

"Of course you'd have more control over those sorts of decisions if you were still sitting on the board, sir."

"They shouldn't call you 'Shark.' They should call you 'Snake.'"

J.J. took a deep breath and looked at the controls, before gazing back out at sea, blinking furiously. To Barrett's horror, he realized the older man was becoming emotional, and instead of feeling the thrill of the kill within his grasp, Barrett's heart clutched, and his first instinct was to reach out and put his arm around J.J. Harrison's shoulder. He didn't, of course, but it occurred to him.

"Fine," rasped J.J. "I'll take the deal, with one caveat."

"Which is?"

"The fishing boat division. I know it's not the most profitable, but it's still in the black every year. Those guys—those craftsmen—have been with me since I was wet behind the ears. I want a guarantee that you don't sever that limb right away. I know it'll be tempting, because it's small and the profits are meager next to the yacht and cargo shop production. But . . ."

"I'll see what I can do," said Barrett.

J.J. nodded, his face in profile a mask of misery as he stared out the massive windows in front of them. "You got what you wanted. Give me a minute, huh?"

He heard the waver in Harrison's voice, noticed the way his fingers fisted around the wood of the ship's wheel until the knuckles were white. Barrett gritted his teeth together. He felt like an asshole. He felt like a murderer.

"It's a good deal, sir," he said quietly, standing up.

"Good for who?" asked J.J., finally looking up at Barrett with watery eyes.

Barrett grimaced lightly before turning to go.

By the time they returned to Trade Winds, the sun was just starting to set and Hélène urged everyone to change for dinner as quickly as possible, advising that they'd be having cocktails at sunset, followed by a cold buffet supper indoors with a local pianist tickling the ivories after dinner.

Emily had noticed the change in Barrett when he returned from his meeting with J.J. Harrison. He was brooding and quiet again, and

Emily was anxious to get back to their room and talk. She'd also made a decision of her own after the beautiful words he'd said to her on the boat, and she was anxious to share that too.

Felicity caught up with them as they walked toward the house slowly, hand-in-hand, bringing up the rear.

"Barrett!" called Felicity. "Tell me again how you know each other? Hélène said it's the most darling story."

"We grew up on the same road."

"Well, I think I know just about everyone who lives on Blueberry Lane. The Storys, the Winslows, the Amblers, and the Rousseaus. Am I missing anyone?"

"The Edwards," said Barrett dryly, holding Emily's hand tighter.

"It just can't be. There are only five houses on your road."

The same concern that Emily'd felt in the car yesterday after playing "Cliché" with Smith surfaced again. He wasn't ashamed of where she came from, was he? His affection for her parents and certainly for her, seemed certain, effortless. But, she couldn't be with him unless she was sure, and now was a unique time to find out once and for all.

"There are actually about fourteen houses on our road," said Emily, glancing at Barrett with worried eyes, relieved to find his face tender and open as he looked down at her. He didn't shake his head no, or flinch, or grimace. Just watched her as though sharing her piece of this puzzle was her choice to make, not his.

Felicity chuckled. "I've lived in Haverford all my life, and I know that—"

"In addition to Haverford Park," Emily interrupted in a calm and level voice, "Green Farms, Westerly, Chateau Nouvelle and Forrester, there are also five gatehouses, three guest houses, and one in-law cottage."

"You just named the five houses, Emily, and you grew up in none of them because I know the people who did. I must be missing your point."

"*People* live in those gatehouses and guest houses, and the late Madame Rousseau lived in the in-law cottage at Chateau Nouvelle until last summer."

"How illuminating."

"I guess it would be if you'd never considered it."

"Gatehouses and guest hou—" Felicity started to scoff, then sucked in a mouthful of air. "Wait . . . Are—are you saying that *you* grew up in a *gate*house or *guest* house?" Her voice was incredulous and her chuckle amused, until Barrett and Emily stopped walking and turned to look at her. Her sparkling eyes were blank with confusion as she stared at Emily, as if seeing her for the first time. "No . . ."

"Yes," said Emily, lifting her chin. "I grew up in the gatehouse at Haverford Park."

"But that can't be. That would mean you're . . . *the help.*" Felicity's jaw dropped, and her glance flicked quickly from Emily to Barrett, then back to Emily again. "You're the daughter of the help?"

"Of the gardener and the housekeeper, yes."

"Oh. Oh, my. Oh, Barrett," said Felicity, her face transformed by mirth. "This is *such* a cliché!"

"*You're* a cliché," he growled, taking a step forward.

"Barrett, don't," murmured Emily, trying to pull his arm back, but finding it as stiff as iron.

"You're a *joke*, Felicity. Thirty-two years old sleeping with a man who has no interest in you. Who's next? J.C. Rousseau? Preston Winslow? We'll just pass you around Blueberry Lane until we're done. How about that?"

Felicity gasped, drawing her arm back to slap Barrett, but Emily intercepted her wrist, holding it firmly and shaking her head. "You won't hit him. He shouldn't have said that, but you started this. You won't hit him."

Felicity wrenched her wrist away with a jerk. "I won't have a *gardener's daughter* tell me what I can and cannot do."

Emily moved slightly to stand in front of Barrett and felt his hands fall onto her hips. She spoke firmly, but gently. "Go back up to the house now, Felicity. This is finished."

Felicity's face turned an interesting shade of purplish-red as she pursed her lips, cutting her eyes from Emily to Barrett. They finally rested on Barrett.

"You'll regret this," she snarled, then turned and stomped up to the house.

Emily reached for Barrett's hand on her hip and sighed as they started walking again.

"We've made an enemy," she observed softly, thinking about what he said earlier about Felicity publicizing the news of Barrett's "engagement" among their mutual social acquaintances. That seemed to be an inevitability now. They'd need to address it at some point, and she'd need to call her parents to tell them it wasn't true to spare them upset.

He shrugged. "I didn't like the way she was talking to you."

"You didn't need to defend me. I'm comfortable with who I am."

"I *didn't* defend you," he answered. "I never even mentioned you. I'm comfortable with who you are, too."

She thought back through his words and realized he was right—he hadn't actually defended her. He'd addressed Felicity and her life, never mentioning Emily at all. He didn't defend her, because he didn't think her life was so lowly that it required defense. The last of her armor slipped away, and the decision she'd made an hour before became final in her mind.

"Barrett," she said softly, dropping his hand so that she could shimmy the engagement ring off her finger. "I'm giving this back."

"What? Why? Because of Felicity? I'm done with her. I haven't been with her since the day I came to see you at Penn."

"*Came* to see me?"

He flinched, biting his lip, shaking his head.

"You bumped into me. After an endowment meeting."

"No, Emily. I didn't have a meeting that day. I came to find you."

"Why? Because you needed a fake fiancée?"

He shrugged. "In part. Also, I overheard your father talking to mine, sharing that he was concerned about your cash flow. I just wanted . . . I just wanted to help you, so I—"

His words were cut off by the feel of her body crashing into his, her hands lacing around his neck. Her lips slammed into his, and her tongue slid into his mouth. He wrapped his arms around her, pulling her up against him in the middle of the lawn, on display for the entire weekend party to see. She didn't care. He had looked after her his entire life, holding her as a baby, bringing her a stuffed bear when she broke her arm, turning his back on a possible engagement because he loved her. Quietly. Not because he wanted fanfare or recognition, but because he loved her. He *loved* her. And she loved him too.

She rested her forehead on his, panting lightly, and let the hand holding the ring twist behind her. When she found his hand, flattened on the small of her back, she peeled the top fingers and dropped the ring in the pouch of palm she had created.

"I'll find another way to get the money for rent," she murmured, feeling drunk and aroused and leveled by the force of her love for him. "I don't want to be your fake fiancée anymore. I want to be your girlfriend. I want to *be* with you, Barrett. Tonight."

"Are you sure?" he asked, his breath soft and hot against her skin.

"I've never been this sure of anything."

He groaned softly, and she felt his fingers close around the ring as he tilted his head and seized her lips again.

Here's what Barrett learned about having to go to a cold buffet and listen to mind-numbingly dull piano music when the woman you're in love with, who happens to be a virgin, tells you she wants you she wants to *be* with you: You are giddily happy that you're actually together for real with no more artifice. You are aroused to the point of discomfort, and at the same time, you're terrified about making everything perfect for her. In short, you're caught between heaven and hell, but there's nowhere else you'd rather be.

He felt so much for Emily, he couldn't bear to let her out of his sight or lose physical contact with her for an instant, keeping his hand in hers, or his arm around her as much as possible. The "in love" part of his brain was on hyperdrive knowing that after a lifetime of longing, he was about to have what he wanted most in the world. All those business partners who counted on "the Shark" for their business transactions would have been staggered by the transformation in Barrett, whose generally aloof personality gave away nothing. With Emily, it seemed, he gave away everything.

Felicity, who had a front row seat to the whipped sap that was Barrett, alternated between shooting them daggers and rolling her eyes from across the room. But for the fact that she was sure to exact her revenge in some potentially embarrassing way for Emily, Barrett couldn't care less. And so what if the world discovered he was "engaged" to Emily Edwards? His friends wouldn't be rude enough to poke around about it until an announcement was made. And if she went to the papers, he'd just give a statement saying that Felicity had blown things out of proportion calling his girlfriend his fiancée, and Felicity would look like a jealous, vengeful ex-lover. Anyway Barrett barely spent a moment thinking about Felicity, he was so mesmerized by Emily, whose eyes had softened with love since giving him back his ring. Was she as anxious to be alone together as he was?

They stood in the back of the room, their hands clasped and laced behind Barrett's back as the pianist launched into a melodic classical piece, and as beautiful as the music was, finally Barrett couldn't stand it anymore. He knew it was poor form to leave before the concert was over, but who would really care? Who would notice if he and Emily quietly slipped away?

He looked down at her head, at the elegant, intricate crown of braids she'd woven in her blonde hair earlier, and squeezed her hand. She looked up at him, her blue eyes clear and luminous. He gestured to the stairs with a slight nod of his head, and watched as her lips tilted up so slightly, anyone else would have missed it. He stepped backwards, pulling her smoothly with him and they tiptoed across the marble hallway to the stairs—which were lit with a flood of moonlight streaming down from a massive skylight—holding her hand until they'd safely closed and locked the door to their room.

Emily stood against their bedroom door, her chest heaving lightly under the silk camisole and light blue tweed jacket she'd been wearing the first night he ever kissed her. Barrett stood facing her from several feet away, his chest mirroring hers, moving up and down rapidly behind the crisp white dress shirt under his tailored dark grey suit. Emily's mind returned briefly to the image of Barrett standing in the bathroom doorway this morning inviting her to take a shower with him. She knew what was under that white shirt and her fingers fisted at her sides, longing for that smooth, hot strength beneath her fingers.

"Do you want me to turn on the lights?" he asked, his eyes dark and languid in the dim light filtering in from outside the window.

She shook her head against the door, wetting her lips and watching as his eyes flicked to her mouth and lingered there.

"Are you okay?" he asked softly, rooted in the same spot.

She nodded, her lips tilting up just a little. He was giving her space, giving her a chance to back out if she'd spoken rashly on the lawn this afternoon.

"Are you nervous?"

"No, Barrett."

"What next?" he asked. His voice was controlled, but she could hear the yearning in it and it spoke to her nerves and told them that he would be gentle and careful with her body and with her heart. "Tell me so I know for sure."

"You," she murmured. "You and me. Together."

He nodded slowly, approaching her, his footfalls muffled by the plush carpet beneath his shoes. When he was within arm's length, he reached out, putting his hands on her hair, finding the pins on either side of her braids and pulling them out carefully. Two French braids dropped to her shoulders, and he trailed his fingers down them, tugging lightly at the elastic bands at the ends. His fingers worked nimbly to release her long blonde hair from the plaits, his eyes holding hers as he worked. When free, he buried his hands in her unusually wavy hair, threading his fingers to the ends, and spreading it over her shoulders like a mantle.

"I've always loved your hair, Emily. It's like sunshine."

His eyes searched her face as he slowly feathered his fingers through the strands from root to tip, the tenderness of his touch relaxing her and exciting her at the same time.

"You and me?" he asked.

"Together," she murmured.

His fingers reached out to unfasten the buttons on her jacket, opening them one by one, without looking down, without releasing her eyes. After the last one, he reached for the lapels and smoothed the jacket over her shoulders, down her arms, letting it drop in a soft heap at her feet.

His fingers played with the delicate cream-colored silk straps of her camisole, the dusting of his fingers on her skin sending shivers down her back. His hands skated down her arms and his fingers tugged lightly at her waist to pull the camisole out of her skirt. She raised her arms, and he lifted it over her head, sucking in a hiss of breath as she stood before him in a strapless white bra and skirt.

"Keep going?" he asked.

"Yes," she said, her heart beating like crazy as her stomach filled with tingles and heat.

His hands landed softly on the bare skin of her waist, then slid to the back her of skirt, finding the zipper and lowering it with a soft *Zzzz* sound. Emily held his eyes, taking one step away from the door and feeling the skirt sluice down her bare legs before pooling on top of the jacket at her feet.

"Jesus," he groaned, dropping her eyes to look at her standing against the door in a white lace bra and panty set, and black high heels.

While he was distracted, she moved her trembling fingers to his shoulders, smoothing them forward, then tucking them under his lapels. He shrugged once and his jacket joined hers on the floor.

"More?" she asked.

His eyes widened, and then his lips tilted up in surprise as he nodded.

"More."

She flattened her palms against his pecs, and he flexed under her fingers, eliciting a small moan from the back of her throat as she slid her fingers to the buttons of his white shirt. He hadn't worn a tie, or buttoned the top button, and the small V of tan skin exposed at the top of his shirt had distracted her all night. She pushed away from the door, and as she unbuttoned his shirt, her lips touched down on the spot at the base of his throat. She felt his breath hitch and hold as her tongue darted out to mark the heat of his skin.

When she drew back, he shrugged the shirt off his shoulders, his eyes dark and smoky as they held hers.

"You and me?" she asked, her fingers reaching for his belt and threading it back through two loops, then pausing. She didn't flinch as the hunger in his eyes beseeched her, wanting her, making her hot and wet in readiness for what was about to happen between them.

"Together," he whispered. His voice was taut and broken, holding on to the last vestiges of his self-control, and it made Emily, a student, a gardener's daughter, a nobody-special, feel like a siren as a shark surrendered to her.

His belt clunked on the growing pile of clothes at their feet, and she unbuttoned and unzipped his pants, hooking her fingers into the waistband and pushing them over his hips. They caught briefly on the jutting bulge in his boxers before hitting the ground in a whoosh. Emily dropped her eyes to the plaid cotton, to the long, hard muscle straining and throbbing against the thin fabric.

She pulled her bottom lip into her mouth as she stared, then lifted her eyes to Barrett. He reached around his neck and pulled off his undershirt, and before she could fully appreciate the beauty of his sculpted chest, his fingers were on the clasp of her strapless bra. With a soft plucking sound, it unfastened and fell to her feet.

She gulped softly, unable to look away from his eyes which flicked down to her chest, flinching, almost in pain, before looking at her face again. His eyes were lost, devastated, devoted, bewildered as he stepped closer to her—so close that her pebbled nipples grazed the hardness of his chest with every shallow breath she took.

"You are *so beautiful* . . . it hurts to look at you."

Her eyes filled with tears as he cupped her face in his hands, his dark, fierce eyes searching hers. Everything that she was, everything she'd always been, belonged to the man holding her so tenderly, and it made her heart swell and throb with love knowing he would be the first man to possess her virgin body, that he would be the person to whom she gave that gift.

"I fell in love with you when I was eight," he whispered.

"Barrett," she breathed, sliding her hands up his arms. "It's always been you."

"Always," he murmured, leaning forward to kiss her. "Always, Emily."

Chapter 13

Barrett ached to throw her on the bed and have his way with her, but since the moment on the lawn when she offered herself to him, he had promised himself, solemnly, to take it slow with her tonight. He was hard to the point of pain, but he was determined not to rush things between them. Emily stepped out of her shoes and moved toward him so that her breasts were flush and full against his chest.

His tongue swept between her lips, and he explored the wet heat of her mouth. His hands slid down her arms to her hands, and he pulled her toward the bed, stepping out of his pants and walking backward carefully. When they got there, she fell onto her back, looking up at him as he quickly pulled off his socks and shoes. His heart pounded as he covered her body with his, the hardness of his hidden erection throbbing against the softness of her thighs, her tight nipples beading into his chest. Every nerve ending fired with longing for her as her back arched beneath him, and her lips sought his again.

He kissed her passionately, thoroughly, swallowing a whimper as she plunged her hands into his hair. Sliding his lips down her neck, he pressed them to her chest, slowly moving to her breast, which he plumped in his hand before dropping his mouth to the erect bud of her nipple. His tongue circled the puckered skin before he sucked greedily, her fingernails grazing his scalp as she bucked into his mouth. He dusted his thumb gently over the swollen nipple before kissing a path to her other breast, which he loved and sucked with the same devotion as he had the first.

"God, Barrett."

She sighed, her response to him making him harder and more impatient for her. The way her hips moved against him, he could tell she was almost ready, but he needed to make sure she was soft and wet before he took her. More than anything, he didn't want to hurt her, or compromise the way she trusted him. He kissed the warm skin under her breasts, sailed his lips over her belly, then leaned back to kneel between her legs, pulling at her panties. She lifted each knee so that he could pull them off, and then she was bared to him. He placed his hand over the trim triangle of soft curls, pushing a little, wanting her to get used to his touch.

"I want to taste you, Emily."

"Please. Yes," she moaned.

He leaned down, gently parting her lips with his fingers, then lowered his head to touch his tongue to the stiff nub of flesh that throbbed for his caress. As he licked and sucked lightly on her sex, her fingers fisted in the sheets by his head, and he chuckled against her sensitive skin, eliciting a gasp as the rumble on his lips vibrated against her core. Gently, he inserted two fingers inside of her, not surprised that she drenched his seeking digits with her wet heat. She arched her back again, and waves of heat flooded his groin making him harder and more swollen than he could ever remember.

He wanted her more than he'd ever wanted anyone, which made her next words the heaven he was hoping for as he gently prepared her for his invasion.

"Barrett," she gasped. "I'm so close, but I don't want to . . . climax without you. I'm ready. Please. I need you."

"Are you sure, baby?" he asked, withdrawing his fingers from her body and sliding up her body to kiss her gently.

She palmed his cheek, her breath touching his lips in pants. "I've always been sure. Please, love."

His eyes fluttered closed for a second at the word "love," and when he opened them, her beautiful face was etched with need. He rolled beside her and pulled down his boxers, kicking them off, then opened the bedside table and pulled out a foil packet, ripping it open and rolling the condom onto his rigid erection.

Bracing himself on his elbows, he covered her body with his and held her head between his hands as he kissed her again, positioning himself at the entrance to her sex. He leaned back to watch her eyes, moving as slowly as he could stand, pushing into her a tiny bit, then waiting. Her eyes widened and her fingers flexed on his back as he pushed forward a little bit more, stretching the tight, wet sheath that sucked him forward.

"More, Barrett."

"God, Emily, I don't want to hurt you."

"You won't," she said softly, her eyes tender and dilated as she gazed up at him. "You've been so gentle, Barrett. So careful. But, I want you. All of you."

"I love you," he whispered, letting go, sliding into her to the hilt.

The combination of him filling her heart at the same time he filled her body was so unexpected, so mind-blowing, she never felt the pain she'd been told she would feel the first time. All she felt was Barrett—his heart beating a primitive rhythm against hers, his sex moving against the walls of hers, his hot breath against her lips as he finally exhaled. In the whole world, there was only Barrett. He was, simply, all that mattered.

She arched up to meet his strokes, feeling a quickening in her stomach that spread through her veins like warm honey, making her fists clench and her toes curl as her ankles slid up his legs and locked behind his back.

The muscles deep inside her body clenched as hard as her fists and toes, tightening to a fevered pitch and as he kissed her. Her eyes rolled back, and she cried out his name, letting the massive wave of pleasure break completely over her. She gasped and shuddered, her muscles squeezing and pulsing around him in a frenzy. Barrett growled her name loudly, thrusting into her one final time. The muscles of his back tightened like steel under her fingertips, and she felt the exact moment he poured himself into the condom, pulsing rhythmically as she had, falling over the edge of bliss to join her.

His breath was hot against her neck as he panted, still deeply imbedded in her body. Emily threaded her fingers through the damp golden waves around his face, and he seemed to rouse himself, taking a deep shuddering breath before rolling to her side.

"Are you okay?" he asked her, still out of breath, leaning up to rest his head on her chest.

"I'm perfect," she whispered dreamily, still brushing his hair off his face with slow, gentle strokes.

"Hold that thought," he said, turning and swinging his legs over the bed to take off the condom and dispose of it before lying back down on his side and pulling her against him, front to front.

Her knees bumped into his and he threaded his legs through hers, resting one arm over her hip, her breasts brushing his chest as they breathed in unison.

He leaned forward and dusted her lips with his, then leaned back to look into her eyes.

"You're definitely okay?"

"Way better than okay. What about you? I was . . . okay?"

"Are you kidding? I'm pretty sure half of the Hamptons just heard me. You were amazing, Emily."

She giggled softly, pressing her forehead to his, nuzzling his nose and sighing contently.

"I'm so happy it was you, Barrett."

"Me too, baby," he said, kissing her nose. "Thank you for trusting me."

They lay quietly side by side until Emily's heavy eyes started fluttering closed as her body matched its breathing to Barrett's. She'd never felt so connected to someone, never felt as cherished as she did by Barrett. All she wanted—for the rest of her life—was to fall asleep next to him every night and see his face first thing every morning. She pictured his face as her brain started to segue to sleep and snuggled closer to him, burrowing her head into his neck and sighing.

"Emily," he whispered near her ear, the rumble of his voice pulling her back from the brink of sleep. "I meant it."

She pressed her lips to his skin and let them linger there.

"I love you," he repeated.

"I love you, too," she whispered.

She felt him gasp quietly, then shudder, and he pulled her tightly against him, as if to let his heart speak to her heart and tell it, *You belong to me, and I belong to you. Always.*

As the morning sun streamed through the windows, Barrett looked over at Emily, his girlfriend, the love of his life, the one woman who'd ever been able to break through his stern exterior to touch his heart. The last three months with Emily appearing regularly in his life had also been the best of his life, despite the fact that he believed she was only answering his calls and joining him for dinner to make a little extra money. To discover that she'd always harbored feelings for him—just as intense, just as deep as his—born, one for the other, in the first days of her life and intractable since, made him breathless, overwhelmed, and . . . *happy.* Really, really happy, such that he'd never known before and would never find again if he lost her. Emily Edwards was it for Barrett. She was the end of the line, the dream come true, his personal forever.

A strand of light hair rested on her cheek, and he gently stroked it away from her face. All he ever wanted—for the rest of his life— was the right to be with her, permission to touch her and take care of her . . . and to love and be loved by her. Every business deal could go to hell, every expectation he'd ever placed on himself or burden he'd carried on his firstborn shoulders—they could only exist in his life if they co-existed with her. She was the only non-negotiable piece of his life now. And eventually—sooner than later—Barrett would ask her the question to make it official. He grinned. After all, he already had the ring.

He swung his legs over the side of the bed, fishing his boxers from the floor and pulling them on. He didn't want to wake her up, but the sun was rising and he could use a run. Although he'd technically closed the deal with J.J. Harrison, it still wasn't sitting right with Barrett. Maybe a run, with fresh air and time for reasoning, would assuage his misgivings, or help him think of an alternative that would sit better.

And if memory served, Felicity was an early riser. Perhaps he could speak with her for a few minutes too, if he caught her getting a cup of coffee. He could apologize for what he said on the lawn and ask for her cooperation in keeping his and Emily's "engagement" a secret. He hoped it was only a matter of time before it was an actuality anyway.

He pulled on his running shorts and a sweatshirt, tugged on athletic socks and sneakers, and with a last look at Emily, he closed the door quietly behind him.

Buzz buzz. Buzz buzz. Buzz buzz.

Her phone was ringing.

Ugh, she thought, drowsily, reaching for it on the bedside table. She clutched it in her hands for a second, but when she heard the *buzz, buzz* sound again, her phone didn't vibrate.

It's Barrett's, it occurred to her, and she rolled to his side of the bed, fishing it off his bedside table to turn it off, opening her eyes groggily.

Just as she reached for it, the buzzes subsided, and Emily started drifting back to sleep with a phone in each hand. She let her mind drift to last night, to all she and Barrett had shared physically and emotionally.

That he was in love with her, she was certain, and her heart assured her that she returned his feelings measure for measure. She had always lusted after Barrett, but more than that, they shared a connection from so long ago. Emily never remembered a time when Barrett hadn't been focal to her life, entrenched in her heart, the first blue eyes that she'd loved. Her dreams swirled and took over, lovely fantasies of Japanese gardens, the fake engagement ring reappearing in Barrett's hand as he knelt before her asking her to be his wife, and she would say—

Barrett's phone made two short dinging sounds and vibrated against Emily's hand.

For heaven's sake! Could it be one of his brothers or could something have happened to one of his parents? Her eyes opened again, and she brought his phone closer to her eyes to read the screen: *New text—Giverny Holdings.*

Giverny Holdings. Valeria's voice echoed in her head: *Giverny Holdings. Does that mean anything to you?* Emily's eyes opened wider and she sat up against the pillow behind her, placing her own phone on the sheet by her thigh and giving her full attention to his. Why would her new landlord, Giverny Holdings, be calling and texting Barrett? How in the world was Barrett even connected to her apartment?

She swiped her finger across the screen, but his phone asked for a passcode. Huh. She tried his birthday. No dice. Then she tried hers, and she ignored the thrill she felt when the screen unlocked. She knew she had no right to look at his private texts, but she couldn't help it. It was too much of a coincidence to ignore.

She tapped her finger on his text app, and waited as a long list of texts came up. She looked briefly over the names: his brothers, of course, J.J. Harrison and other names she didn't recognize. But, it was the name on the top of the list that commanded her attention: Giverny Holdings. She tapped on the newest text which read:

> Barrett, I can't get this chick, Valeria Campanile, off my back. She keeps calling and threatening to track down the articles of incorporation for the shell company if I don't give her the name and phone number of the landlord. She's going to find you if she keeps digging. What do you want me to do? Pls. advise.

Emily's eyes zoned out as Barrett's phone dropped from her hand onto the sheets pooled in her lap. A lump was forming in her throat and her cheeks were feeling that uncomfortable tingling when she knew something was wrong, but hadn't quite put all the pieces together.

Barrett was her landlord.

Barrett had raised her rent, knowing that she'd be forced her to go back to work for him.

Her eyes burned and her fingers felt cold as she curled them into fists.

What did it mean? She demanded that her brain start putting pieces together to figure out what was real and what wasn't. Were his feelings for her real? Did he really love her? Her heart clutched, but she forced herself to calm down. Emily was not given to wild fits of pique. She was sensible, smart and methodical and she was going to take an overview approach to this situation, just as she did to her studies, and figure out what was going on.

She took a deep breath, sorting out her thoughts quickly, picking up his phone to check his texts again and see when J.J Harrison had invited them to the Hamptons. She found the text sent on Friday night while she was in the hospital with her mother, and the pieces starting fitting together quickly.

He'd needed her to come with him this weekend.

He'd needed her to continue being his "fiancée" for the sake of J.J. and Hélène Harrison.

He'd needed her to do that so that his deal could close.

So he'd raised her rent on Friday night and showed up at her parent's house on Saturday afternoon to offer her the job back . . . or to see if she'd ask for it. Which she had. Devious and manipulative? Check. But, fairly straightforward too.

Having untangled the fake fiancée/business side of things, she turned her thoughts to more personal matters. Their conversations, their attraction and feelings . . . Emily sensed strongly that his feelings for her existed apart from his machinations to have her in attendance this weekend. And while she didn't appreciate being manipulated, she suspected Barrett wasn't as smooth in relationships as he was in the boardroom. Instead of asking for her help, he'd purposely—and a bit deviously—controlled the situation to get the outcome he wanted.

Unfortunately for him, however, Emily wouldn't be able to put up with this sort of thing if they were to continue dating one another. She didn't want to be at the mercy of Barrett pulling strings in her life without her knowledge. She couldn't live like that, and she fumed a little, feeling angry with him for his jockeying and manipulations and not just telling her the truth and trusting that she would help him because he needed her and she cared for him. She knew how much business meant to Barrett and how good he was at it—but she couldn't allow him to apply his boardroom tactics to their relationship.

She took a deep breath, steeling herself for the frank—and potentially devastating—conversation they needed to have the moment he returned. Either he needed to treat her with respect and honesty, or there could be no future for them, and her heart winced at the mere idea of losing him. Tears pricked her eyes as she thought about walking away from him after what they'd shared last night, but she thought of her own parents—their easy communication and implicit trust—that's what Emily wanted, and she wouldn't accept anything less.

Her attention was stolen by the door to their room opening and Emily flicked her eyes up, tugging the sheet under her armpits and placing both phones on her lap. As Barrett's eyes landed on her face, they took her breath away, and for a brief moment, she forgot about Giverny Holdings and her apartment and his manipulations. Whatever conniving he'd been up to for the sake of his business deal, the same eyes that had held hers twenty-four years ago told her that he loved her today, told he that he was deeply and irrevocably *in love* with her and that those feelings were real and true and strong. Her shoulders drooped a little with relief as her heart calmed a bit from its fierce racing.

"Good morning, Emily," he said, standing at the edge of the bed, grinning at her. "I love you."

"Morning, Barrett," she answered, raising one eyebrow while her anger made her voice lower, harder and less playful than he probably expected. "I love you, too. But I'm afraid you have some 'splainin' to do."

His eyes flicked down to the two phones in her lap, then back up to her face, noticing—for the first time—that her eyes weren't bright and happy, but disappointed and hurt. His stomach flipped over and he searched her expression, sitting down on the edge of the bed. She scooted slightly away from him and his heart caught. What was going on?

"Giverny Holdings," she said clearly. "Tell me about that."

"Fu—" Barrett sighed, clenching his jaw and shaking his head. She'd found out. Goddamnit, she'd found out before he could fix it. "Emily—"

"You know what, Barrett? Actually, I think I figured it out. You needed me here this weekend, because the Harrisons had invited us to come together. Somehow you're my landlord, which is slightly creepy—but so very you—and you decided to raise my rent so I'd need another job from you. So far, so good?"

He nodded tightly, bile rising in the back of his throat. Like all dealmakers, Barrett's thoughts beelined to the bottom line. What did this mean for them? Did it mean that she'd break up with him? His heart literally stopped working for a moment, pausing for several seconds before beating again. He couldn't lose her. That was not an acceptable outcome.

"So, I asked for a job, you offered the Hamptons. Voila, fake fiancée back in line for a weekend and lo and behold, your deal goes through."

He stared at her, feeling wide-eyed and terrified but trying to keep his face impassive, bracing for her to break up with him—and yes, he deserved it—and frantically telling himself that even if she did, he wouldn't give up. She could break up with him, but he wouldn't let her go. He'd find a way to get her back. He'd—

"Barrett, focus on what I'm saying."

"I'm sorry."

"That's a good start," she replied, but her eyes were still hurt and her lips were still pursed. Her hands were laced tightly in her lap, and she looked down at the phones. "I don't generally look at people's phones, but it kept buzzing and when Giverny Holdings came up, I . . . well, I was curious because Valeria had already mentioned the name to me. I didn't know how you were connected and it felt like I needed to know."

"Don't apologize to me."

Her eyes narrowed briefly, and her voice cracked like a whip when she replied, "I'm not apologizing for anything."

His cheeks flushed. "Excellent. Fine. Good."

"Barrett," she asked, locking her eyes with his. "Why do you own my apartment building?"

He shrugged. "It was a good investment."

Her eyes widened at him and she huffed, not even dignifying his answer with a verbal response. She just stared at him, waiting.

"Because I asked your Mom for your address so I could track you down, and your apartment's in a crappy neighborhood, and I wanted to upgrade the security system, but when I offered to pay the landlord to upgrade it, he told me to screw myself. So I asked what it would take to upgrade it, and he said I'd have to own the building to make those sorts of demands, so I bought it."

He felt juvenile and manipulative, exposed and embarrassed.

"And you didn't just bump into me at Penn after an endowment meeting."

"I already came clean on that one. I was looking for you."

"Did you even *need* a fake fiancée?"

"I'd been doing okay without one, though the meetings all went better once you were sitting next to me." He grimaced, understanding her need for total and complete honesty and anxious to offer it. "No. I didn't need one. I didn't want you to worry about money, and I didn't know how else to offer you a job."

It was all true. Just having her beside him made him feel invincible. If she was next to him, he couldn't lose. He couldn't.

But more than anything, he couldn't lose *her*, and he couldn't help but feel like that's where the conversation was headed: him confessing to multiple manipulations and her finally giving him the boot once everything had been revealed. *I'll get her back. I'll get her back. I'll die before giving up on us—*

"So we'll call that one a *partial* manipulation?"

He shrugged, miserable. All he'd really wanted was to be around her, to find out if it was finally time for them to give each other a chance after a lifetime of waiting. And it was. It *had* been. They'd fallen for each other so effortlessly, he knew that what he'd suspected since childhood—that they were meant for each other—was true.

"And this? Forcing me to come to the Hamptons by raising my rent?"

"The Harrisons wanted you here. And I—"

"Wanted the deal to go through."

"No. Well, yeah. But I wanted you here too. Even more than I wanted the deal, Emily, I wanted *you*." He swallowed the lump in his throat.

She took a deep breath, tilting her head to the side, considering him. "We've worked out the business end of things, I think. I don't like it, but I get it. Now I need the rest, Barrett. The truth about you and me and everything that's happened between us. I need to know if this—if everything personal that happened between us—was part of you manipulating me . . . or if it was real."

Chapter 14

He reached for her hands, and she let him take them because as she figured things out with him, she'd never seen him look so helpless, so miserable, so desperate. And while a very, very small part of her was glad he was so worried, the reality was that she loved him, and she couldn't bear to see him so undone.

But she was angry with him, and they wouldn't be able to move forward until they sorted everything out. Now.

"Isn't it exhausting to be you, Barrett? To do anything for the deal? Manipulate me? Manipulate J.J.?"

"I didn't—"

"You did. You threatened him and manipulated him. Just like you did me."

He flinched, holding her fingers more tightly. She knew she was hurting him with her words, but she plowed forward. These things needed to be said.

"I'm not even mad that you bought my building or messed with my rent. You're Barrett English. You're used to getting your own way, and mostly I'm okay with that. It's part of who you are—it's part of what makes you so successful and protective, and I love those things about you, Barrett. Know what I *don't* love?"

His eyes were fraught as he held hers, listening carefully and respectfully to her words.

"You manipulated me instead of talking to me, instead of being honest with me and just explaining the situation and asking for my help. That's what hurts me most of all, because I was honest with you. Always. About everything except the Riesling."

His eyes softened for a moment at her lighter reference, and she saw the hope there behind the worry. She was glad because it meant he was listening to her and really hearing her.

"I'm worried that you treat your personal life with the same determined, single-minded, outcome-driven focus that you do your business life . . . and that just won't work for me. You can't lie to me, Barrett. You can't manipulate me when you want something from me. I love it that we made love last night, but I don't like it that you lied to get me here in the first place. Lying and manipulating *me* will make cracks in *us*. And I don't want cracks. I need to be with someone who talks to me, who's honest with me and cares about my opinions. Who asks me for help when he needs it. Who trusts I want what's best for him, and wants what's best for me. That's the kind of love I want, Barrett. And right now, I don't know if you can offer that to me. I'm worried that you can't."

His face contorted for a moment before settling into granite, his hands holding hers so tightly his knuckles were white. She'd said her piece. She took a deep breath and sighed, signaling him that she was finished, that she'd said everything she needed to say.

He looked down at their joined hands for a long moment before seizing her eyes again, but his voice broke as he said two words. "I can." He gulped softly, then continued. "You asked if this was real . . . This is the most real thing in my life. *You're* the most real thing in my life, Emily."

Tears sprang to her eyes, but she didn't interrupt him. It was important for her to hear what he had to say, to know that they were going to build the rest of their relationship on honesty and partnership, or not at all.

He sniffed once, then cleared his throat before continuing in a stronger voice.

"The truth is that I bought your building to keep you safe. I offered you the job with me because I knew you needed money, and once I started spending time around you again, I started falling for you . . . as an adult. A man falling for the woman of his dreams, the woman he wants in his life forever. I just didn't know if you had any feelings for me.

"The night at dinner with the Harrisons when you reached for my hand and started weaving that story about us actually being engaged? That was the touchstone, Emily, the turning point. That was the moment I realized it didn't just have to be a dream. It was possible. After a lifetime of wanting you, *you* were finally possible, Emily.

"I admit it. I panicked. You gave me back the ring, and yes, technically I knew the Harrison deal would have a better chance if you were here. But, more than anything else, getting you to come here this weekend was about me wanting time with you. I needed to spend time with you and figure out if what happened in the car was a one-shot deal or the start of something real, because I knew what I wanted, but I still wasn't sure about you.

"When you told me why you'd given me back the ring—because we'd gotten physical and you couldn't take money from me anymore—I thought about throwing the deal just so I could have you. No deal. No fake fiancée. Dump the deal and ask you to be my girlfriend.

"But I guess I stupidly hoped I could have both . . . except I'm sitting here beside you and the deal feels all wrong, and I'm not sure if I've already lost you, but, God, I hope not. Because I will do *whatever* it takes to make this right, Emily. If that means full disclosure about everything going on in my life, all the time? That's fine. I can do that. I will never, ever keep anything from you. Never again. I promise you. I know I screwed this up, but just give me a chance to show you I can be whatever you need me to be, whatever you want me to be."

He raised her hand to his lips and kissed it slowly and gently. There was "good-bye" in that kiss and longing and hope. Emily felt all of it, and it took all of her strength not to rush to reassure him, but let him finish saying everything he needed to say. He lowered their hands to his lap and searched her eyes.

"In the interest of full disclosure? The ring you've been wearing isn't a fake. It's worth thirty grand. I had that Chanel suit custom-made to match your eyes and you're so beautiful in it, I can't breathe. If you'd let me, I'd knock out your rent altogether, but I know you won't, so I'm going to send a text right now to lower it by one-thousand dollars indefinitely to make up for worrying you and making you think—for even a second—that you had to move.

"And yes, for the record, I manipulated you to get you here, but I slept with you last night because I love you." He gasped softly, taking a deep breath before continuing. "I have *always* loved you. You were a tiny baby and I was a little boy and you reached into my chest and stole my heart, and it's been yours ever since. You're home and sweetness and truth and brilliance and you're sexy and teasing and the most fun I ever had. And if you want to know what's real, here's the most elemental truth I know: You're the love of my life, Emily Edwards. And whatever it takes, I'll do it. Just to be with you."

Tears streamed down Emily's cheeks as he finished his beautiful speech, staring at her face with his stunning blue eyes that were fixed on hers unflinchingly, worried and hopeful.

"Barrett," she started, dropping his hands to reach for his face, a beaming smile cutting through her tears. "Don't you ever do things in half measures?"

"No."

She nodded, and felt laughter bubble up from deep inside of her—joyful, delighted laughter born of requited love and satisfied longings. She pulled him to her, pressing her lips to his. He was still tense for a moment before he sighed into her mouth, letting go of his fears and sinking into her forgiveness and understanding. He wrapped his arms around her with a growl, hauling her against his chest as his tongue pressed into her mouth, finding hers, loving it gently, then desperately, all the feelings he'd just poured into his words now manifesting themselves physically. He reached for his shirt behind his neck and ripped it from his body, pressing his hot, damp chest against her breasts as the sheet slipped between them, leaving them skin to skin, heart to heart.

And as they climaxed together moments later, and Barrett told Emily he loved her, there was no part of her heart, or soul, or mind left wondering if it was true. She knew it was. As surely as the sky was as blue as Barrett English's eyes, she knew that she would be his forever, and he would love her until the end of time.

Emily rested her head on Barrett's chest after the most mind-blowing orgasm of his life, and he gently stroked her back.

"Remember when you asked me about great sex?"

"Mm-hm," she murmured and he felt her lips tilt up against his skin.

"I didn't know what I was talking about when you asked."

"No?"

"No. Definitely not. I had never experienced great sex. Not until last night. Not until this morning."

He concentrated on what she was drawing on his chest. Hearts. *I love you. I'm yours.* He kissed the top of her head reverently, pulling her closer.

"I'm the best you ever had, huh?" she asked in a saucy voice that made him hard again.

"If I get my way, you'll be the last I'll ever have."

"Barrett?" she asked in a tentative voice.

"What, baby?"

"We need to date for a little while."

His heart clutched, but he knew she was right. Her finger moved slowly. Deliberately. *It's okay. I'm yours.* He took a deep breath, resting his lips on her head again.

"Okay," he finally murmured, accepting her terms. "But I want to give you something."

He swung his legs over the side of the bed and grabbed the pants he'd been wearing last night, rummaging through the pockets, then lying back down on his side, propped up on his elbow over her. He held up the engagement ring and she blanched. Then he placed it on the warm skin over her heart and wrote above it with his finger. *Don't worry. You decide.*

She leaned up on her side to face him and the ring fell between them on the sheets. "What does that mean?"

"It means I want to marry you and I'm not going to change my mind so I don't need more time. But it's okay that you do. So, you keep it and we'll date for a little while. And one day, when you're ready, if you're ever ready, put it on." He grinned at her. "Until then, don't lose it."

"I won't," she whispered, picking it up and putting it on her right pinkie. "It's beautiful, you know."

"I know," he said, staring at her face. "There's nothing more beautiful in the whole world. I love you. Forever."

Emily pushed him gently onto his back and proceeded to show him exactly how much she loved him too.

"Before we go," Emily said, packing up the rest of her things after they'd made love again and taken a long shower together, "I think you should talk to J.J. Harrison, Barrett. Business isn't all about business. It can't be, because there are people involved. And people mean history and heart. You said yourself that this deal feels all wrong. Why? And what can you do to make it right?"

He glanced at her from across the room, considering her words. "I don't know. There's something about Harrison . . . how much he loves this company. Most of the time, when I take over a corporation, it's already publicly-held, so English & Sons buys up the stock and once we have a majority, we're in charge. I don't like taking over privately held companies because they're messier. Brothers and sisters and infighting. This looked pretty straightforward, to be honest. Five siblings. Four wanted to sell. Get the fifth to agree, and we're in like Flynn. We acquire the most lucrative privately held yacht and cargo ship business on the east coast. It was a no-brainer."

"You didn't count on J.J. Harrison."

Barrett shook his head, remembering the old man's steel grey eyes watering as they came to a grudging agreement on the boat yesterday. He was offering J.J. Harrison approximately seventy million dollars for his thirty percent stake in Harrison Shipbuilding and all Harrison could think about was the dinky fishing boat arm of the company. Of the two hundred and forty-seven million dollars in annual sales, only eighteen million came from the fishing boats.

"What kind of business man cares about the fishing boats?" Barrett asked aloud.

"What? What do you mean?"

"Harrison stands to make seventy million dollars on this deal, but all he talked about yesterday was this little division of the company that makes fishing boats locally, here on Long Island. They don't even account for ten percent of the annual profits. Honestly, my first order of business would have been to shut it down, but he asked that I didn't."

"Why does it mean so much to him?"

Barrett shrugged, zipping his suitcase closed and taking it off the luggage rack to wheel it over to the door. "Something about his grandfather making fishing boats by hand."

"Barrett," said Emily softly. "Don't you see? That's the answer."

"I don't—"

"To make it all okay. Let him keep that part of his company. It's the part that matters to him. Figure out a way for him to keep it so that he can protect it."

Barrett's mind worked the numbers quickly. With sales of eighteen million dollars over the past fiscal year, the little fishing boat operation was probably only worth twenty million dollars. Small potatoes. But, Emily might be right—letting Harrison keep one small division would not only keep Barrett from feeling like such a scumbag, but J.J. Harrison would probably be more likely to take a board position for the independent cargo and yacht building company.

He'd text Fitz and Weston to draw up a new contract that provided for J.J. Harrison keeping the fishing boat division of Harrison Shipbuilding and for English & Sons to acquire the cargo and yacht divisions. Barrett was pretty sure J.J. would happily agree to sit on the board now. Barrett's heart felt lighter, too, like this was a good deal now, a deal he could be proud of.

"Emily?" he asked, crossing the room to put his hands on her hips and pull her up against his chest. "Did you ever think about getting your MBA instead?"

She grinned at him. "I'll stick to the *history* of industry and leave the *present-day* deal making to you, okay?"

He dropped his lips to her neck, and she tilted her head to give him better access. "You know, Emily Edwards, I think we might just be a match made in heaven."

"No Barrett," she murmured, her voice low with want as he kissed and licked her, and Barrett knew it would be another hour, at least, before they left their room. "We were made on earth, you and me. In your parent's living room. Twenty-four years ago."

While Barrett went in search of J.J. Harrison, Emily waited for him in the sitting room, sipping coffee and flipping through a magazine. She'd already said her good-byes to Hélène, who had left for church services, and the house was so quiet Emily assumed everyone else had already departed too. She was surprised to hear footsteps and looked up to see Felicity Atwell standing before her.

"Mind if I sit?" asked Felicity.

"That depends."

Felicity gave Emily a very tight smile, but unless she was misreading it, it wasn't mean. Uncomfortable, yes. Calculating, no.

"Barrett looks happy," said Felicity softly, her blue eyes direct as they held Emily's.

"Barrett *is* happy."

"I think . . . I think I hoped he might be *the one*. I'd always been ga-ga for Barrett, since he asked me to dance the foxtrot at Mr. West's Dancing School. And then we ended up at Penn together. When I ran into him at the Union Club a couple of years ago, I thought: Now's the time! This is finally going to happen! And it did, I guess, for a while."

Emily didn't know what to say. She knew that Felicity was part of Barrett's past, and she was rational about him having previous lovers, but picturing them together was painful. She kept her face carefully neutral, hoping Felicity would get to the point.

"The thing is . . . Barrett was never really available. Not really. I guess the closest I ever saw to him falling in love was with Bree Ambler, but he was even reserved with her. With you? He's riveted, transfixed . . . in love, I think, for the first time in his life."

Emily knew what Felicity was saying was true, because she'd never seen Barrett look at anyone the way he looked at her, either. She knew that what she had with Barrett was a forever love, and the ring in her pocket scorched a hole to her heart. *Not yet*, she whispered to it. *Not yet*.

"I had no right to say those things to you yesterday. To make fun of you for being the gardener's daughter. It's unconventional, I guess, but if anyone can pull it off, it's Barrett." Felicity sighed, then offered Emily the first genuine smile Emily had seen all weekend. "We'll move in the same circles now. I'd like for us to be friends."

Felicity held out her hand and Emily took it, smiling back at the older woman who had just admitted defeat with grace and dignity.

"Thank you, Felicity. I'd like that, too." Emily let go of Felicity's hand and straightened in her chair. "He didn't mean it. What he said yesterday."

"Oh, yes he did. And you know? He was right. If I'm not careful, I'll miss the boat on the rings because I was having so much fun in the beds. Maybe it's time for me to grow up a little bit, too."

Felicity stood up, smoothing her simple cotton eyelet sundress and dropping her sunglasses from her head to her eyes. "There was a patent lawyer here, and if I'm not mistaken, he's still lingering around somewhere. Off to the hunt."

Emily chuckled lightly and gave Felicity the thumbs up sign as her erstwhile rival sashayed out to the patio to find her next victim.

An hour later, in the car on the way to the small Hamptons airport, Barrett told Emily all about his conversation with J.J. Harrison: how the old man's eyes had brightened at the thought of keeping the fishing boat business. In fact, he declared, it was the perfect retirement project and with all of his attention focused on building quality handmade boats, maybe they'd consider segueing into sailboats too. Barrett had chuckled and asked if J.J. was taking on investors.

"No more deals with you, Shark. I've learned my lesson."

"Fair enough, sir."

"If you don't mind my saying, that girl you're with? She's very good for you. She softens your edges, just like Hélène does for me. Every man needs a good woman at his side, English. We're lost without them."

At his side, thought Barrett. *A partner.*

"So it all worked out," said Emily, her broad smile reaching her shining eyes as stunning mansions and pristine beaches raced by on either side of the car.

Barrett glanced at Emily and thought of how close he came to losing her, of how much he loved her, of how his children would have her blue eyes and blonde hair, and the Edwards and English families would see another generation grow up running around the grounds of Haverford Park, racing from the gatehouse to the main house because it would all belong to them.

He took her hand and raised it to his lips, then smiled into the eyes of the woman he'd always loved, whom he would love forever.

"It all worked out, baby."

THE END

The English Brothers continues with . . .

FALLING FOR FITZ

THE ENGLISH BROTHERS, BOOK #2

THE ENGLISH BROTHERS
(Part I of the Blueberry Lane Series)

Breaking Up with Barrett
Falling for Fitz
Anyone but Alex
Seduced by Stratton
Wild about Weston
Kiss Me Kate
Marrying Mr. English

Turn the page to read a sneak peek of *Falling for Fitz*!

Chapter 1

Fitzpatrick English walked into the ballroom at the Hotel Dupont
in Wilmington, Delaware, stood in the doorway and sighed. Unlike
Barrett, Alex and Weston, three of his four brothers, who all enjoyed
a night out with the best of Main Line society, Fitz wasn't much of
a fan of these sorts of gatherings. All things equal, he'd just as soon
be at home watching college football in sweats and drinking a cold
beer.

He envied his younger brother, Stratton, who had declined invita-
tions to these sorts of events for so long, no one even asked anymore.
Stratton was probably at home in his den-like penthouse, feet up on
the coffee table, glass of merlot half-finished and some terrific book
on his Kindle. Stratton probably didn't even own a tux anymore. Fitz
put a finger into the starched white collar of his shirt and wiggled it
slightly. *Best just get it over with.*

"Hello, second-born."

An arm was suddenly laced through his and he looked down to
find his mother, Eleanora Watters English, beaming up at him.

"Evening, Mom."

"It's lovely you showed up. I know these things aren't your favorite."

Fitz sighed. "Barrett has a way . . ."

"Barrett has *always* had a way. However, I will say that the last two
months have been void of his usual intensity over business, swapped
for his intensity over Emily Edwards. It's been a refreshing change,
though if she keeps him waiting for an answer for much longer, he will
get trying."

As Eleanora led them through the crowd toward the table Barrett had purchased for the 23rd Annual Kindred Hospital Harvest Call Fundraiser, Fitz caught sight of his older brother. Barrett always looked like James Bond in a tux, while Fitz always felt like a penguin. Barrett had his arm wrapped around Emily's waist, as they talked to another couple who had their backs to Fitz. Occasionally Barrett would look down and smile at Emily, and Fitz almost blushed at the intensity in his brother's gaze. Fitz could barely remember feeling that way about someone. It had only been for such a short time, so long ago, sometimes he thought it had all been a dream.

"Usual cast of characters tonight?"

"Not exactly. The English have been invaded . . . by the Edwards," she said, forced humor thick in her manicured voice. Although she never voiced concerns about her oldest son seriously dating the daughter of the gardener with an eye to engagement, Fitz suspected his mother had had some initial misgivings. However, from the way she looked at Barrett and Emily now, it seemed those misgivings had been exchanged for acceptance. Emily made Barrett happy, and in the end, that would trump anything else where his mother's sensibilities were concerned. Though mixing it up socially with one's help wasn't exactly commonplace, if anyone could pull it off with panache, it was Eleanora English.

Fitz looked over the heads of a few guests to see Susannah and Felix Edwards sitting at the table, Felix in animated conversation with his father, Tom, and Susannah talking tête-à-tête with Weston, who was probably untangling some crisis of the heart with their beloved housekeeper.

"I assume nine and ten are Alex and whomever he brought with him tonight?"

"No, dearest." Eleanora stopped them a few feet from the table, and turned to look at Fitz, her eyes careful, but searching. "I did say an *invasion* by the Edwards. Felix and Susannah wouldn't exactly constitute an invasion."

Fitz stared at his mother's face, not understanding her meaning. "But there are no other Edwards . . . Felix, Susannah and Emily, that's all—"

Suddenly he jerked his head around to look at the couple Barrett and Emily were talking to. From behind, the woman had long, straight blond hair, just like Emily's, that ended in the center of her bare back. He narrowed his eyes, squinting, and he made out the light brown birthmark that looked like a heart, right in the center of her lower back, right over the midnight blue silk that covered her perfect ass. He had a sudden, blinding flashback to staring at that birthmark over tiny, bright yellow bikini bottoms, and his heart kicked into a gallop.

"Daisy Edwards," he murmured, exhaling the contents of his lungs.

And as though she heard him or sensed him, Daisy turned her neck, catching sight of him as her chin rested on her shoulder. His heart slammed behind his ribs as she blinked in surprise and her eyes widened. Their eyes stayed locked on each other, spellbound and greedy, until Emily said something to Daisy, and she jerked back quickly to face her cousin. The ten or twelve feet apart from her was suddenly unbearable and as though Fitz was made of iron and she was a magnet, he felt pulled to her in an uncompromising way, compelled to move closer to the force of nature that was Daisy Edwards.

His mother's arm, still linked with his, stopped him.

"It was a million years ago, Fitz."

It didn't feel like a million years ago. Suddenly it felt like yesterday.

"It was for the best," insisted Eleanora.

It didn't feel like it had been for the best. Not at the time and not now and not every time he thought of her between then and now.

"I thought she was in Oregon," he said tightly.

"She was. She's moved back east. Her mother's gone and her father's all she has."

"So she's back in Philly. Did you know?"

"No," replied his mother. "I didn't even know she was coming tonight. Emily invited her at the last minute when Stratton refused to come."

His breath caught as Daisy gathered her hair in her hands and twirled it once, then settled it over one shoulder, baring her neck to him. The graceful line made his mouth water, made his fingers twitch, made a hundred buried memories fight for his attention.

"Listen to me, Fitz," said his mother, leaning closer to his ear. "There's something else you need to know."

Fitz tore his eyes away from Daisy and looked at his mother, commanded by the seriousness of her tone. "You may not have noticed, but she isn't alone."

He whipped his head around and for the first time he noticed that the man standing beside her was holding her hand, with his fingers laced possessively through Daisy's. His mother's voice was close to his ear and delivered the words he somehow knew were coming, though it didn't lessen the impact of the blow.

"She's come home for another reason, dearest. Daisy's getting married."

Look for *Falling for Fitz* at your local bookstore or buy online!

Other Books by Katy Regnery

A MODERN FAIRYTALE
(Stand-alone, full-length, unconnected romances inspired by classic fairy tales.)

The Vixen and the Vet
(inspired by "Beauty and the Beast")
2015

Never Let You Go
(inspired by "Hansel and Gretel")
2015

Ginger's Heart
(inspired by "Little Red Riding Hood")
2016

Don't Speak
(inspired by "The Little Mermaid")
2017

Swan Song
(inspired by "The Ugly Duckling")
2018

ENCHANTED PLACES
(Stand-alone, full-length stories that are set in beautiful places.)

Playing for Love at Deep Haven
2015

Restoring Love at Bolton Castle
2016

Risking Love at Moonstone Manor
2017

A Season of Love at Summerhaven
2018

ABOUT THE AUTHOR

USA Today **bestselling author Katy Regnery** started her writing career by enrolling in a short story class in January 2012. One year later, she signed her first contract for a winter romance entitled *By Proxy*.

Katy claims authorship of the multi-titled Blueberry Lane Series which follows the English, Winslow, Rousseau, Story and Ambler families of Philadelphia, the five-book, bestselling A Modern Fairytale series, the Enchanted Places series, and a standalone novella, *Frosted*.

Katy's first Modern Fairytale romance, *The Vixen and the Vet,* was nominated for a RITA® in 2015 and won the 2015 Kindle Book Award for romance. Four of her books: *The Vixen and the Vet* (A Modern Fairytale), *Never Let You Go* (A Modern Fairytale), *Falling for Fitz* (The English Brothers #2) and *By Proxy* (Heart of Montana #1) have been #1 genre bestsellers on Amazon. Katy's boxed set, The English Brothers Boxed Set, Books #1–4, hit the *USA Today* bestseller list in 2015 and her Christmas story, *Marrying Mr. English*, appeared on the same list a week later.

Katy lives in the relative wilds of northern Fairfield County, Connecticut, where her writing room looks out at the woods, and her husband, two young children, and two dogs create just enough cheerful chaos to remind her that the very best love stories begin at home.

Sign up for Katy's newsletter today: http://www.katyregnery.com!

Connect with Katy

Katy LOVES connecting with her readers and answers every e-mail, message, tweet, and post personally! Connect with Katy!

Katy's Website: http://katyregnery.com
Katy's E-mail: katy@katyregnery.com
Katy's Facebook Page: https://www.facebook.com/KatyRegnery
Katy's Pinterest Page: https://www.pinterest.com/
    katharineregner
Katy's Amazon Profile: http://www.amazon.com/
    Katy-Regnery/e/B00FDZKXYU
Katy's Goodreads Profile: https://www.goodreads.com/author/
    show/7211470.Katy_Regnery